PENGUIN CLASSICS
THE CONFUSIONS OF YOUNG TÖRLESS

Robert Musil was born in Klagenfurt, Austria, in 1880. After abandoning military school he trained as a mathematician, behavioural psychologist, engineer and philosopher. His first novel, *The Confusions of Young Törless*, an early example of expressionistic writing drawing on his experience of military school, appeared in 1906. During the First World War he served as an officer in the Austrian Army on the Italian front. Having distinguished himself as a soldier, Musil forsook brilliant opportunities and chose, instead, to retire into his writing. His other works include the short stories of *Three Women* (1924) and a play, *The Enthusiasts* (1921). He is perhaps best known for his great novel, *The Man without Qualities* (1930–43), which established Musil as one of the great German writers of the twentieth century, whose work has been compared to Rilke and the Expressionists. This reputation, however eluded him during his lifetime. His small private income was lost in the German inflation and he emigrated from Berlin, and then Vienna, in order to escape Nazism. He died exiled and impoverished in Switzerland in 1942.

Shaun Whiteside was born in Dungannon, Northern Ireland, in 1959, and educated in Dungannon Royal School and King's College, Cambridge, where he graduated with a First in Modern Languages. He has translated widely from German, French and Italian, and his translations of Arthur Schnitzler's *Beatrice and Her Son* and Friedrich Nietzsche's *The Birth of Tragedy* are published by Penguin.

J. M. Coetzee was born in Cape Town, South Africa, in 1940, and educated in South Africa and the United States. His highly acclaimed books include *Life & Times of Michael K* (1983), winner of the 1983 Booker Prize and the 1985 Prix Etranger Femina; *The Master of Petersburg* (1994), which was awarded the *Irish Times* International Fiction Prize, and *Disgrace* (1999), winner of the 1999 Booker Prize.

THE CONFUSIONS
OF YOUNG TÖRLESS

ROBERT MUSIL

TRANSLATED FROM THE GERMAN BY SHAUN WHITESIDE

WITH AN INTRODUCTION BY J. M. COETZEE

PENGUIN BOOKS

PENGUIN BOOKS

Published by the Penguin Group

Penguin Group (USA) Inc., 375 Hudson Street, New York, New York 10014, U.S.A.

Penguin Group (Canada), 90 Eglinton Avenue East, Suite 700, Toronto,
Ontario, Canada M4P 2Y3 (a division of Pearson Penguin Canada Inc.)

Penguin Books Ltd, 80 Strand, London WC2R 0RL, England

Penguin Ireland, 25 St Stephen's Green, Dublin 2, Ireland (a division of Penguin Books Ltd)

Penguin Group (Australia), 250 Camberwell Road, Camberwell,
Victoria 3124, Australia (a division of Pearson Australia Group Pty Ltd)

Penguin Books India Pvt Ltd, 11 Community Centre, Panchsheel Park, New Delhi – 110 017, India

Penguin Group (NZ), cnr Airborne and Rosedale Roads,
Albany, Auckland 1310, New Zealand (a division of Pearson New Zealand Ltd)

Penguin Books (South Africa) (Pty) Ltd, 24 Sturdee Avenue,
Rosebank, Johannesburg 2196, South Africa

Penguin Books Ltd, Registered Offices: 80 Strand, London WC2R 0RL, England

Die Verwirrung des Zöglings Törleß first published 1906
This translation published in Penguin Classics (UK) 2001
Published in Penguin Books (USA) 2001

Introduction copyright © J. M. Coetzee, 2001
Copyright © Rowholt Verlag GmbH, 1978
Translation copyright © Shaun Whiteside, 2001
All rights reserved

CIP data available
ISBN 0 14 21.8000 9

Set in Janson

Introduction

Robert Musil was born in 1880 in Klagenfurt, capital of the Austrian province of Carinthia. His mother, who came from the upper bourgeoisie, was a highly strung woman with an interest in the arts. His father was an engineer in the imperial administration who in his later years would be rewarded for a career of faithful service with elevation to the minor nobility. Musil Senior accepted without protest a liaison between his wife and a younger man, Heinrich Reiter, that began soon after his son's birth. Reiter later settled in with the Musils, in a *ménage à trois* that endured for a quarter of a century.

Musil himself was an only child. Younger and smaller than his classmates at school, he cultivated a physical toughness that lasted all his life. His home life seems to have been tempestuous; at the demand of his mother – and, it must be said, with the boy's enthusiastic agreement – he was sent at the age of eleven to board at a military *Unterrealschule* outside Vienna. From there he moved in 1894 to the *Oberrealschule* in Mährisch-Weisskirchen near Brno, capital of Moravia, where he spent a further three years. This school became the model for 'W.' in *Young Törless*.

Rather than follow a military career, Musil decided to study engineering, and at the age of seventeen enrolled in the *Technische Hochschule* in Brno, where his father now taught. Here he plunged into his scientific studies, disdaining the humanities and the kind of student attracted to the humanities. His diaries reveal him as preoccupied with matters of sex, but in unusually thoughtful ways.

He found it difficult to accept the sexual role prescribed for him as a young man by the mores of his class, sowing his wild oats with prostitutes and working girls until it was time to make a bourgeois marriage. He began a relationship with a Czech girl named Herma Dietz who had worked in his grandmother's house; against the resistance of his mother and at the risk of losing his friends, he lived with Herma in Brno and later in Berlin. Choosing Herma constituted a major step in breaking the erotic spell his mother had over him. For some years Herma was the focus of his emotional life. Their relationship – straightforward on Herma's side, more complex and ambivalent on Robert's – became the basis of the story 'Tonka', collected in *Three Women*.

In intellectual content, the education Musil had received at his military schools was decidedly inferior to the education offered by the classical *Gymnasia*. In Brno he began attending lectures on literature and going to concerts. What began as a project in catching up with his better-educated contemporaries soon turned into an absorbing intellectual adventure. The years 1898 to 1902 mark the first phase of Musil's literary apprenticeship. He identified particularly with the writers and intellectuals of the generation that flowered in the 1890s, active in various strands of the Modernist movement. He fell under the spell of Mallarmé and Maeterlinck; he rejected the naturalist premise that artwork should reflect a pre-existing reality. For philosophic support he turned to Kant, Schopenhauer and (particularly) Nietzsche. In his diaries he developed the artistic persona of 'Monsieur le vivisecteur', exploring states of consciousness and emotional relations with his intellectual scalpel, practising his skills impartially on himself, his family and his friends.

Continuing, despite his literary aspirations, to plan for a career in engineering, he passed his examinations with distinction and moved to Stuttgart as a research assistant at the prestigious *Technische Hochschule*. But his work there bored him. While still writing technical papers, and inventing an instrument for use in optical experiments (he patented the device, hoping, rather unrealistically, that it would provide him with enough money to live on), he embarked on a novel, *The Confusions of Young Törless*. He also began to lay the ground for a change in academic direction; in 1903 he finally abandoned engineering and left for Berlin to study philosophy and psychology.

Young Törless was completed in early 1905. After it had been turned down by three publishers, Musil sent it to Alfred Kerr, a respected Berlin critic. Kerr lent Musil his support, suggested revisions, and reviewed the book in glowing terms when it appeared in print in 1906. Despite the success of *Young Törless*, however, and despite the mark he was beginning to make in Berlin artistic circles, Musil felt too unsure of his talent to commit himself to a life of writing. He continued with his philosophical studies, taking his doctorate in 1908.

By this time he had met Martha Marcovaldi, a woman of Jewish descent seven years his senior, separated from her second husband. With Martha – an artist and intellectual in her own right, *au fait* with contemporary feminism – Musil established an intimate and intensely sexual relationship that lasted for the rest of his life. They were married in 1911, and took up residence in Vienna, where Musil had accepted the position of archivist at the *Technische Hochschule*.

In the same year Musil published his second book, *Unions*, consisting of the novellas 'The Perfecting of a Love' and 'The Temptation of Quiet Veronika'. These short pieces were composed in a state of obsessiveness whose basis was obscure to him; writing and revision occupied him day and night for two and a half years.

When war came, Musil served with distinction on the Italian front. After the war, troubled by a sense that the best years of his creative life were slipping away, he sketched out no fewer than twenty new works, including a series of satirical novels. A play, *The Visionaries* (1921), and a set of stories, *Three Women* (1924), won awards. He was elected vice-president of the Austrian branch of the Organization of German Writers. Though not widely read, he was on the literary map.

Before long the projected satirical novels had been abandoned or absorbed into a master project: a novel in which the upper crust of Viennese society, oblivious of the dark clouds gathering on the horizon, discusses at length what form its next festival of self-congratulation should take. The novel was intended to give a 'grotesque' (Musil's word) vision of Austria on the eve of the World War. Supported financially by his publisher and by a society of admirers, he gave all his energies to *The Man without Qualities*.

The first volume came out in 1930, to so enthusiastic a reception in both Austria and Germany that Musil – a modest man in other respects – thought he might win the Nobel Prize. The continuation proved more intractable. Cajoled by his publisher, yet full of misgivings, he allowed an extended fragment to appear as the second volume in 1933. He began to fear he would never complete the work.

A move back to the livelier intellectual environment of Berlin was cut short by the coming to power of the Nazis. He and his wife returned to the ominous atmosphere of Vienna; he began to suffer from depression and poor health. In 1938 Austria was absorbed into the Third Reich. The couple moved to Switzerland. Switzerland was meant to be a staging-post *en route* to a home offered by Martha's daughter in the United States, but the entry of the United States into the war put paid to that plan. Along with tens of thousands of other exiles, they found themselves trapped.

'Switzerland is renowned for the freedom you can enjoy there,' observed Bertolt Brecht. 'The catch is, you have to be a tourist.' The myth of Switzerland as a land of asylum was badly damaged by its treatment of refugees during World War Two, when its first priority, overriding all humanitarian considerations, was not to antagonize Germany. Pointing out that his writings were banned in Germany and Austria, Musil pleaded for asylum on the grounds that he could earn a living as a writer nowhere else in the German-speaking world. Though allowed to stay, he never felt at home in Switzerland. He was little known there; he had no talent for self-promotion; the Swiss patronage network disdained him. He and his wife survived on handouts. 'Today they ignore us. But once we are dead they will boast that they gave us asylum,' remarked Musil bitterly to Ignazio Silone. Depressed, he could make no headway with the novel. In 1942, at the age of sixty-one, after a bout of vigorous exercise on the trampoline, he had a stroke and died.

'He thought he had a long life before him,' said his widow. 'The worst is, an unbelievable body of material – sketches, notes, aphorisms, novel chapters, diaries – is left behind, of which only he could have made sense.' Turned away by commercial publishers, she privately published a third and final volume of the novel, consisting of fragments in no hard and fast order.

Musil belonged to a generation of German intellectuals who experienced the successive phases of the breakdown of the European order between 1890 and 1945 with particular immediacy: first, the premonitory crisis in the arts, giving rise to the various Modernist reactions; then the war and the revolutions spawned by the war, which destroyed both traditional and liberal institutions; and finally the rudderless post-war years, culminating in the Fascist seizure of power. *The Man without Qualities* – a book to some extent overtaken by history during its writing – set out to diagnose this breakdown, which Musil more and more came to see as originating in the failure of Europe's liberal élite since the 1870s to recognize that the social and political doctrines inherited from the Enlightenment were not adequate to the new mass civilization growing up in the cities.

To Musil, the most stubbornly retrogressive feature of German culture (of which Austrian culture was a part – he did not take seriously the idea of an autonomous Austrian culture) was its tendency to compartmentalize intellect from feeling, to favour an unreflective stupidity of the emotions. He saw this split most clearly among the scientists with whom he worked, men of intellect living coarse emotional lives. The education of the senses through a refining of erotic life seemed to him to hold the most immediate promise of lifting society to a higher ethical plane. He deplored the rigid sexual roles that bourgeois mores laid down for women and men. 'Whole countries of the soul have been lost and submerged as a consequence,' he wrote.

Because of the concentration in his work, from *Young Törless* onwards, on the obscurer workings of sexual desire, Musil is often thought of as a Freudian. But he himself acknowledged no such debt. He disliked the cultishness of psychoanalysis, disapproved of its sweeping claims and its unscientific standards of proof. He preferred a psychology of what he ironically called the 'shallow' – that is, experimental – variety.

Both Musil and Freud were in fact part of a larger movement in European thought. Both were sceptical of the power of reason to guide human conduct; both were diagnosticians of *fin de siècle* Central European civilization and its discontents; and both assumed the dark continent of the feminine psyche as theirs to explore. To Musil, Freud was a rival rather than a source.

His preferred guide in the realm of the unconscious was Nietzsche ('master of the floating life within', as he called him). In Nietzsche Musil found an approach to questions of morality that went beyond a simple polarity of good and evil; a recognition that art can in itself be a form of intellectual exploration; and a mode of philosophizing, aphoristic rather than systematic, that suited his own sceptical temperament. The tradition of fictional realism had never been strong in Germany; as Musil developed as a writer, his fiction became increasingly essayistic in structure, with only perfunctory gestures in the direction of realistic narrative

Die Verwirrungen des Zöglings Törless (*Verwirrungen* are perplexities, troubled states of mind; *Zögling* is a rather formal term, with upper-class overtones, for a boarder at a school) is built around a history of sadistic victimization at an élite boys' academy. More specifically, it is an account of a crisis that one of the boys, Törless (his first name is never given), experiences as a result of participating in the deliberate humiliation and breaking down of a fellow student, Basini, who is caught stealing. The exploration of this inner crisis, moral, psychological, and ultimately epistemological, rendered largely from within Törless's own consciousness, makes up the substance of the novel.

In the end Törless has his own breakdown and is discreetly removed from the school. Törless's sense is that he has weathered the storm and come through. But it is not clear how far we are intended to trust his newfound confidence, since it seems to be based on a decision that the only way of getting along in the world is not to peer too closely into the abysses opened up in us by extreme experience, particularly sexual experience. The single glimpse we are allowed of Törless in later life suggests that he has become not necessarily a wiser or a better man, merely a more prudent one.

In later life Musil denied that *Young Törless* was about youthful experiences of his own, or even about adolescence in general. 'The reality one is describing is always only a pretext,' he said, meaning (one presumes) that the action of the novel was simply a vehicle to allow him to explore a certain state of mind. Nevertheless, the originals of Basini and of his tormentors Beineberg and Reiting can easily be identified among the boys Musil knew at Mährisch-Weisskirchen, while one of Törless's deepest confusions – about the nature of his feelings towards his mother – is mirrored in Musil's own early diaries. The gap between Törless's own outward sang-froid and the seething forces within him, between the well-regulated daily life at school and the eerie nocturnal floggings in the attic, has its parallel in the gap between the orderly bourgeois front presented by Törless's parents and what he darkly knows must go on in the privacy of their bedroom.

The master metaphor that Musil uses for all these incommensur-abilities comes from Törless's studies in mathematics. Living side by side with the real numbers, and somehow made to interlock with them by the operations of mathematical reasoning, are the imaginary numbers, numbers which have no referent in the real world. Adults, led by Törless's teachers, seem to have no trouble in bringing together the domains of the real and the imaginary (to Törless the vertiginously unimaginable). In the euphoric speech he makes to the assembled teachers at the end of the book, Törless claims to have resolved this confusion in his mind ('I know that I was indeed mistaken') and to have emerged safely into young adulthood ('I'm not afraid of anything any more. I know: things are things and will remain so for ever'). His teachers understand nothing of what he says: they have either never had experiences like his, or have tightly repressed them. Törless is unusual in the thoroughness with which he has faced – or been driven to face – the darkness within; whether or not we regard as self-betrayal his later adoption of the pose of what Musil as narrator calls the 'aesthetically inclined intellectual', he is certainly, in his confused youth ('confusion', *Verwirrung*, is a word Musil uses with continual irony), the figure of the artist in the modern world, exploring the remoter shores of experience and bringing back his reports.

Despite the amoralism that makes *Young Törless* so much a product of its age, the moral questions raised by the story will not go away. Beineberg, the more intellectually inclined of Törless's comrades, has a vulgar-Nietzschean, proto-Fascist justification for what they do to Basini: the three of them belong to a new generation to which the old rules do not apply ('the soul has changed'); as for pity, pity is one of the lower impulses and must be conquered. Törless is not Beineberg. Nevertheless, his own particular perversity – making Basini talk about what has been done to him – is morally no better than the whippings the other two carry out; while in his own homosexual acts with Basini he is at pains to show the boy no tenderness.

In a world in which there are no more God-given rules, in which it has fallen to the philosopher-artist to give the lead, should the artist's explorations include acting out his own darker impulses, seeing where they will take him? Does art always trump morality? This early work of Musil's offers the question, but answers it in only in the most uncertain way.

Musil did not disown *Young Törless*. On the contrary, he continued to look back with surprise at what he had been able to achieve, even at a technical level, at so early an age. The master metaphor of the book, with its implication that the foundations of our real, reasonable, everyday world have no real, reasonable existence, continues to be explored in *The Man without Qualities*, though in a spirit more of paradox and irony than of anguish. 'A person must believe he is something more in order to be capable of being what he is,' suggests Ulrich, the central character. 'The present is nothing but a hypothesis that one has not yet finished with.' Musil's work, from beginning to end, is of a piece: the evolving record of a confrontation between a man of supremely intelligent sensibility and the times that gave birth to him, times he would justly call 'accursed'.

'As soon as we put something into words, we devalue it in a strange way. We think we have plunged into the depths of the abyss, and when we return to the surface the drop of water on our pale fingertips no longer resembles the sea from which it comes. We delude ourselves that we have discovered a wonderful treasure trove, and when we return to the light of day we find that we have brought back only false stones and shards of glass; and yet the treasure goes on glimmering in the dark, unaltered.'

–Maeterlinck

A little station on the stretch leading towards Russia.

Infinitely straight, four parallel iron tracks ran in both directions, between the yellow gravel of the wide track. Alongside each, like a dirty shadow, was the dark line burned into the ground by the exhaust.

Behind the low, oil-painted station building a wide, rutted road led down to the ramp. Its edges faded into the flat-trodden ground all around it, and could only be identified by two rows of acacia trees standing on either side, their parched leaves asphyxiated by dust and soot.

Whether it was these sad colours, or whether it was the wan, faint light of the afternoon sun, exhausted by the haze: there was something indifferent, lifeless, mechanical about both objects and people, as though they had been taken from the stage of a puppet theatre. From time to time, at regular intervals, the station manager stepped out of his office and, each time with an identical turn of his head, looked up the broad stretch of track to the signals of the guard's hut, which still failed to announce the approach of the express train that had been subject to a long delay at the border; then, with the same movement of his arm he drew out his pocket watch, shook his head and disappeared again; like the coming and going of the figures that step out of old church clocks to announce the hour.

On the wide, well-trodden strip between the rails and the build-ings a cheerful party of young people was taking a stroll, walking on either side of an elderly couple who formed the centre of the rather loud conversation. But even the merriment of the group was not genuine; the sound of hearty laughter seemed to fall silent after a few paces, sinking to the ground as though it had encountered some stubborn and invisible obstacle.

Behind her dense veil, Frau Törless – this was the lady of about forty – hid eyes that were sad and red from crying. She was saying goodbye. And once again it was hard for her to leave her only child among strangers for so long, unable to watch over her darling herself.

For the little town was a long way from their home, in the eastern part of the Empire, in the midst of dry and sparsely populated farm land.

The reason why Frau Törless had to bear the fact of her son being in such remote and inhospitable foreign parts was that the town was home to a famous boarding-school built the previous century on the site of a religious foundation. Since that time it had been left where it was, probably to protect the growing adolescents from the corrupting influences of a big city.

For it was here that the sons of the country's best families received their education, to go on to university after they left the institute, or to join the army or the civil service. For all of these purposes, as well as for social contact in the circles of respectable society, it was thought to be a particular advantage to have been educated at the seminary in W.

Four years previously these considerations had led Herr and Frau Törless to yield to their son's ambitious urgings and arrange for him to receive a place at the school.

This decision had later cost many tears. Because almost since the moment when the door of the institute had shut irrevocably behind him, little Törless suffered from terrible, passionate homesickness. Neither lessons, nor games in the lush, spacious meadows of the park, nor the other distractions offered by the school, held his attention; he barely took part in them. He saw everything as though through a veil, and during the day he often had trouble choking back a persistent sob; but at night he always cried himself to sleep.

He wrote letters home, almost every day, and he lived only in those letters; everything else that he did seemed to him only a shadowy, meaningless set of events, indifferent stages like the marks on a clock face. But when he wrote he felt something distinctive, exclusive within him; like an island full of wonderful suns and colours, something surged up within him out of the sea of grey sensations that crowded around him with cold indifference day after day. And if by day, at games or in class, he remembered that he would write his letter in the evening, he felt as though he was wearing, hidden on an invisible chain, a golden key with which, if no one was looking, he would be able to open a gate into the most wonderful gardens.

The strange thing about it was that he found something new and alarming in this sudden, consuming affection for his parents. He had never previously been aware of it, he had happily gone to the institute of his own free will, indeed he had laughed when his mother had been unable to contain her tears at their first farewell, and only after he had been alone for a few days and felt comparatively at ease did it suddenly surface in him with elemental force.

He thought it was homesickness, a longing for his parents. But actually it was something much more vague and complex. Because in fact it no longer contained the 'object of that longing', the image of his parents. I mean that three-dimensional memory, not merely mental but physical as well, of a loved one, which addresses all the senses and is stored in all the senses, in such a way that one can do nothing without feeling the other person's presence, silent and invisible, at one's side. This memory soon died away like an echo that has gone on reverberating for only a short while. Törless could no longer, for example, call up the image of his 'dear, dear parents' – as he usually thought of them – before his mind's eye. Whenever he tried to do so, a boundless pain welled up within him in its place, torturing him with its yearning and yet holding him under its spell, because its hot flames both pained and delighted him. More and more, the thought of his parents became a mere pretext for generating within himself that egoistic suffering which enfolded him in its voluptuous pride as though he were in a secluded chapel where, surrounded by hundreds of flaming candles and hundreds of eyes of holy images, incense is strewn among the flagellants intent on their self-inflicted torture.

Then, when his 'homesickness' became less violent and gradually faded away, this trait of his grew quite apparent. The disappearance of his yearning did not bring with it any long-awaited contentment, but left a void in the soul of young Törless. And in that nothingness, that incompleteness, he recognized that what he had lost was not merely longing but something positive, a spiritual strength, something that had blossomed and faded within him under the cover of pain.

But now it was over, and that source of a first superior bliss had made itself known to him only by running dry.

Now the passionate traces of his awakening soul vanished once more from his letters, to make way for detailed descriptions of life in the institute and the new friends he had made.

He himself felt impoverished and bare, like a tree experiencing its first winter after a fruitless blossoming.

But his parents were contented. They loved him with a strong, unthinking, animal tenderness. Whenever he had holidays from the boarding-school, his mother felt the house was empty and deserted again after he left, and she would walk through the rooms with tears in her eyes for days after those visits, here and there caressing an object on which the boy's eyes had rested, or which his fingers had held. And both of his parents would each have allowed themselves to be torn to pieces for his sake.

The clumsy emotion and passionate, defiant grief in his first letters painfully preoccupied them and sent them into a state of fraught hypersensitivity; the cheerful, contented thoughtlessness that followed made them happy again as well, and, feeling that a crisis had been averted, they supported him to the best of their abilities.

In neither of these states did they recognize the symptom of a particular spiritual development. Instead they had seen both their son's pain and its abatement as being more or less a natural consequence of the prevailing conditions in the school. They failed to see that this was their son's first unsuccessful attempt, thrown upon his own devices, to develop his own inner strength.

Törless was very discontented now, and groped around in vain for something he might use as a support.

One episode from this time was characteristic of what was being prepared within Törless, to develop further at a later stage.

One day young Prince H., a member of one of the most influential, oldest and most conservative aristocratic families in the Empire, joined the school.

Everyone else found his gentle eyes sentimental and affected; they mocked as effeminate the way he jutted one hip out when he stood, and played slowly with his fingers when he talked. But they particularly derided him for having been brought to the boarding-school not by his parents, but by his former teacher, a doctor of theology and a member of a religious order.

But he had made a very strong impression on Törless from the first. Perhaps the fact that he was a prince and thus presentable at court had something to do with it. At any rate Törless was now meeting a very different kind of person.

The aura of devotional practices and the silence of an old aristocratic castle seemed somehow to linger around the prince. When he walked, it was with soft, lithe movements, with that contraction of the body that goes together with the habit of walking erect through a suite of empty halls, where anyone else would seem to bump into unseen corners in the empty space.

Keeping company with the prince thus became a source of refined psychological pleasure for Törless. Dawning within him was the kind of knowledge of human nature that teaches us to know and appreciate another person by the fall of his voice, the way he picks something up, even the timbre of his silence and the expression of the physical posture with which he occupies a space; in short, by that agile way, barely tangible and yet the only truly complete way, of being something spiritual and human, which is layered around the tangible, effable core as around a bare skeleton, and by means of that appreciation to anticipate his mental personality.

During this brief time Törless lived as though in an idyll. He did not take exception to his new friend's religious nature, which was actually something quite alien to him, coming as he did from a free-thinking, bourgeois family. Instead he accepted it without further ado, indeed he even considered it a peculiar distinction on the prince's part, because it intensified that person's essence, which he felt to be so dissimilar to his own as to be beyond comparison.

In the prince's company he felt as though he were in a chapel some distance from the beaten track, where the idea that he didn't really belong there vanished in the face of the pleasure of seeing daylight through stained-glass windows and letting his eye glide over the useless, gilded decoration that had accumulated in the boy's soul until he had a vague picture of that soul, as though he were drawing with his finger a beautiful arabesque which made no sense to him but which looped according to unknown rules.

Then the two boys suddenly fell out.

It had been a blunder, as Törless would later have to admit.

They had been arguing about religious matters. And that moment had been the end of everything. Because, as though it was quite independent of him, Törless's intellect had lashed out at the gentle prince. He heaped upon him the ridicule of the rationalist, like a barbarian he smashed the filigree structure in which the boy's soul was housed, and they parted in anger.

Since that time they had not spoken a word to one another. Törless was dimly aware that he had done something idiotic, and a vague, emotional insight told him that the wooden ruler of rationalism had shattered something fine and delightful at an untimely moment. But that was something entirely outside his power. A kind of longing for the past remained with him, and probably would for ever, but he seemed to have entered a different stream, which was carrying him further and further away from it.

And then, after a while, the prince, who had not been happy there, left the school.

Now Törless's world became very empty and boring. But he had grown older in the meantime, and the first signs of sexual maturity were beginning, slowly and darkly, to well up within him. During this stage of his development he formed some new friendships commensurate with his age, which would later be of very great importance to him. With Beineberg and Reiting, with Moté and Hofmeier, the very same young people with whom he was today accompanying his parents to the railway station.

Curiously, they were the worst of his year, talented and, obviously, of good family, but sometimes wild and unruly to the point of brutality. And if it was their company that now held Törless enthralled, this was probably due to his own lack of independence, which had grown very severe since his break with the prince. It could even be seen as a direct continuation of that changed direction, because, like it, it signified a fear of excessively subtle sentimentalities; and with such feelings the nature of his other classmates formed a healthy, sturdy, life-embracing contrast.

Törless yielded entirely to their influence, because his intellectual situation was more or less this: by his age, at a Gymnasium, one will have read Goethe, Schiller, Shakespeare, perhaps even the modern authors. That reading re-emerges, half-digested, through the fingertips. Roman tragedies are produced, or terribly sensitive lyrical effusions which stride across whole pages, as though dressed in the finest and most delicate lace: things which are inherently ridiculous, but which have an inestimable value for the soundness of a young person's development. For these associations and borrowed emotions, coming as they do from outside, carry young people over the dangerously spongy spiritual ground of the years during which one must signify something to oneself, while one is still too incomplete really to signify anything at all. It is of no consequence whether anything remains of this, or whether it does not; for each of us comes to terms with himself, and the only danger lies in the transitional age. If one were to make a young person aware of how ridiculous he was, the ground would swallow him up, or else he would plummet like a sleepwalker who has been awoken, and who suddenly sees nothing but the void.

That illusion, that trick favouring personal development, was missing from the institute. For although the library contained the classics, these were thought to be boring, and otherwise it held nothing but volumes of sentimental short stories and supposedly humorous tales of the military life.

Young Törless had read his way through the lot in his greed for books, and some tritely tender notion from one short story or another would sometimes linger with him for a while, but it had no influence, no real influence, on his character.

It seemed at the time as though he had no character whatsoever.

Under the influence of this reading, for example, he himself wrote the occasional little story or began the occasional romantic epic. So excited was he about the amorous sufferings of his heroes that his cheeks blushed, his pulse quickened and his eyes gleamed.

But when he set aside his pen it was all over; in a sense his mind lived only in motion. So he was also able to jot down a poem or a story at any time, in response to any stimulus. It excited him, but he never took it entirely seriously, and the activity did not strike him as important. Nothing of it entered his character, and it did not spring from it either. It was only in response to some external compulsion that he had any sensations beyond indifference, just as an actor needs the compulsion that a role imposes upon him.

These were cerebral reactions. But that which we take to be a person's character or soul, his inner line or colour, compared to which his thoughts, decisions and actions, being of little significance, appear random and interchangeable – that which had, for example, brought Törless together with the prince in the face of all rational judgement – that fixed, final backdrop, was entirely lacking in Törless at this time.

In his classmates it was the enjoyment of sport, an animal quality, that meant they had no need of such a thing, a gap filled, in the Gymnasium, by play with literature.

But Törless was too intellectual for the former, and for the latter, life in the institute, which required that its pupils be constantly ready to engage in quarrels and fist-fights, made him too sensitive to the absurdity of such borrowed emotions. Thus his nature assumed a certain vagueness, an inner helplessness, which meant that he could not find out where he was.

He attached himself to his new friends because he was impressed by their wildness. Since he was ambitious he tried every now and again to outdo them. But each time he stopped half-way, and suffered a certain amount of ridicule as a consequence. He would then feel intimidated again. His whole life during that critical period really consisted only in his repeated attempts to emulate his rough, more masculine friends, and at the same time in a deep and inward indifference towards his own efforts.

Now, when his parents visited him, he was quiet and shy while they were on their own. He drew away from his mother's tender caresses, always under a different pretext. He would really have loved to yield to them, but he was ashamed, as though his classmates' eyes were upon him.

His parents took it as the awkwardness of the developing years.

In the afternoon the whole noisy horde would turn up. They played cards, ate, drank, told anecdotes about the teachers and smoked the cigarettes that the Hofrat* had brought from the capital.

This merriment pleased the couple and put their minds at rest.

They did not know that times could sometimes be different for Törless. And, recently, that was true more and more often. There were moments when life in the institute left him utterly indifferent. Then the putty of all of his day-to-day worries dissolved, and the hours of his life fell apart with no internal connection.

Often he sat for a long time – in gloomy reflection – hunched over himself, so to speak.

This time, as usual, the visit had lasted two days. They had eaten, smoked and gone on an outing, and now the express train was to bring the couple back to the capital.

A quiet rumble in the rails announced its approach, and the signals of the bell on the roof of the station building rang relentlessly in the ear of Frau Törless.

'Isn't that right, my dear Beineberg? You will look out for my boy for me?' Hofrat Törless turned towards young Baron Beineberg, a tall, bony lad with sticking-out ears, but with expressive, clever eyes.

Little Törless pulled a face at such presumption, and Beineberg grinned, both flattered and enjoying his friend's discomfort.

'Generally speaking,' – the Hofrat turned to the others – 'I should like to ask you all to let me know if anything were to happen to my son.'

This drew from young Törless an infinitely bored: 'But, Papa, what could happen to me?' But he was used to letting this excess of concern wash over him every time they said goodbye.

The others, in the meantime, clicked their heels, drawing their elegant swords stiffly to their sides, and the Hofrat added, 'You can never know what lies ahead, and the idea of being immediately

---

* An honorific title, 'Court Councillor', for senior officials in the Imperial administration.

informed of anything would be a great consolation to me; after all, my son, you might not be in a position to write.'

Then the train pulled in. Hofrat Törless embraced his son, Frau von Törless pressed her veil tighter to her face to hide her tears, the friends took their leave one by one, and then the guard shut the coach door.

For one last time the couple saw the high, bare rear façade of the institute building – the massive, long wall surrounding the grounds, and then on both sides there were only greyish-brown fields and the occasional solitary fruit tree.

In the meantime the young people had left the station and were walking two abreast on either side of the road – in that way they avoided at least the densest and harshest of the dust – towards the town, without saying a great deal to one another.

It was past five o'clock, and a cold, grave atmosphere was falling across the fields, a harbinger of evening.

Törless became very sad.

Perhaps it was down to his parents' departure, although perhaps it might only have been the dull, chilly melancholy that now lay heavily upon the whole of the surrounding landscape, and even as little as a few paces away blurred the shapes of objects with heavy, lacklustre colours.

The same terrible apathy that had lain upon everything all afternoon now crept towards him over the plain, and behind it, like a slimy trail, the mist that clung to the newly ploughed land and lead-grey turnip fields.

Törless looked neither right nor left, but he could feel it. Step after step he placed his feet in the tracks that the boy ahead of him had made in the dust – and that was how he felt things were: as if this was how they had to be: a stony compulsion that captured and compressed the whole of his life into this movement – one step after the other – along this single line, along this narrow strip running through the dust.

When they stopped at a crossing, where a second path met their own in a circular patch of firmly trodden earth, and when a ramshackle signpost loomed crookedly into the air, that line, forming such a contrast with its surroundings, had the effect on Törless of a cry of desperation.

Again they walked on. Törless thought of his parents, of acquaintances, of life. At that time of day people were dressing for a party or deciding to go to the theatre. And afterwards they would go to the restaurant, listen to a band, visit a café. One would meet an interesting person. A romantic adventure would keep one in a state of expectation until the morning. Life keeps rolling out new and unexpected things like some marvellous wheel . . .

Törless sighed at this thought, and with each step that brought him closer to the confinement of the institute something inside him twisted tighter and tighter.

Now the bell was ringing in his ears. He feared nothing as much as that bell, which announced the end of the day once and for all – like a brutal knife slash.

He wasn't having any experiences, he reflected, and his life was fading away in perpetual apathy, but that bell added a note of mockery, and made him tremble with impotent fury about himself, his fate, the buried day.

From this point on you can experience nothing at all, for twelve hours you will experience nothing, for twelve hours you are dead . . . That was what the bell meant.

When the party of young people reached the first low, hut-like houses, that dull brooding fled from Törless. As if seized by sudden interest, he raised his head and strained to see into the hazy interior of the dirty little buildings they were passing.

At the doors of most of them stood women, in aprons and coarse shirts, with broad, dirty feet and bare brown arms.

If they were young and sturdy, they called out some coarse Slavic jibe, nudged each other and giggled about the 'young gentlemen'.

Sometimes one of the girls cried out, if someone had brushed her breast too hard in passing, or replied with a laughing insult to a slap on the thigh. Some of them only watched after the rushing boys with serious and angry expressions; and if he happened to have joined them, the farmer would smile in embarrassment, half unsure of himself, half good-natured.

Törless didn't join in with the high-spirited, precocious manliness of his friends.

The reason for that probably lay partly in a certain shyness where sexual matters were concerned, common to almost all only children, but it lay more in his particular kind of sensual temperament, which was more hidden, more powerful and darker in tone than that of his friends, more severe in its expression.

While the others pretended to be shameless with the women, almost more in order to appear 'smart' than out of any real desire, the soul of silent little Törless was churned up and lashed by genuine shamelessness.

He looked through the little windows and warped, narrow doorways into the interiors of the houses with such a burning gaze that it was as though a fine net was constantly dancing before his eyes.

Nearly naked children rolled about in the mud of the farmyards, here and there the skirt of a working woman revealed the backs of her knees, or a heavy breast pressed stiffly into the canvas folds of her shirt. And, as though all of this was taking place in a quite different, animal, oppressive atmosphere, there flowed from the hallways of the houses a sluggish, heavy air, which Törless greedily inhaled.

He thought of old paintings he had seen in museums without really understanding them. He was waiting for something, just as he had always waited, when looking at such paintings, for something that had never happened. For what . . . ? . . . Something surprising, something he had never seen; a terrible sight that he could not even imagine; something with a terrible, animal sensuality, something that would grip him as though with claws and tear him to pieces beginning with his eyes; an experience that must have something to do, in a way that was still far from clear to him, with the dirty pinafores of the women, with their rough hands, with their low-ceilinged rooms, with ... with the farmyard filth ... No, no ... the only thing he could feel now was the fiery net before his eyes; the words didn't capture it; it isn't nearly as bad as words make it seem; it's something quite mute – a choking in the throat, a barely perceptible thought – and only if one really wanted to say it with words would it come out like that. But even then it bears only a remote resemblance, as though in a vast enlargement, in which one not only sees everything more clearly, but even things that aren't there ... And yet it was something to be ashamed of.

'Is the little one homesick?' The sudden, mocking question came from von Reiting, tall and two years older, who had noticed Törless's silence and gloomy eyes. Törless gave a false and embarrassed smile, and he felt as though the malicious Reiting had been listening in to what had been going on within him.

He didn't reply. But by now they had reached the little town's cobbled church square, where they parted.

Törless and Beineberg did not yet want to go back to the institute, while the others had no permit to stay out any longer and went home.

The two of them had stopped off at the café.

There they sat at a little round-topped table beside a window looking out on to the garden, beneath a gas chandelier whose lights hummed quietly behind their milky glass spheres.

They had made themselves comfortable, they had their glasses filled with different kinds of schnapps, smoked cigarettes, ate some pastries in between and enjoyed the contentment of being the only guests. For if there was anyone else there at all, it was someone sitting on his own over a glass of wine in one of the back rooms;

here at the front it was quiet, and even the fat, elderly owner seemed to have fallen asleep behind her counter.

Törless looked – just vaguely – through the window – out into the empty garden, which was gradually getting darker.

Beineberg was telling stories. About India, as usual. Because his father, who was a general, had been there as a young officer in the service of the English. And he had not only, like other Europeans, brought back carvings, weavings and little manufactured idols, he had also sensed and retained something of the bizarre and mysterious half-sleep of esoteric Buddhism. Whatever he had learned there and later added to by reading he had passed on to his son, from his childhood onwards.

His way of reading was peculiar. He was a cavalry officer and had no great love of books in general, holding novels and philosophy equally in contempt. If he read, he did not want to read about opinions and contentious issues; rather, when he opened books he wanted to step as if through a secret portal into the midst of the rarest insights. They had to be books the mere possession of which was like the secret sign of an order, and like a guarantee of unearthly revelations. And that he found only in books of Indian philosophy, which did not seem mere books to him, but revelations, reality – key works like the alchemical texts and the magic books of the Middle Ages.

This healthy and active man, who carried out his duties to the letter and also managed to ride his three horses almost every day, locked himself in with those books, usually towards evening.

Then he would select a passage at random and ponder whether its most secret meaning might this time be revealed to him. And he had never been disappointed, however often he had to concede that he had penetrated no further than the forecourt of the consecrated temple.

So something like an aura of solemn mystery floated around this wiry, tanned, outdoor man. His conviction that he was on the threshold of a shatteringly great revelation early each evening gave him a reserved superiority. His eyes were not dreamy, but calm and hard. Their expression had been formed by his habit of reading books in which not a single word could be displaced without disturbing its esoteric significance, by carefully and attentively reading each sentence for its meaning and double meaning.

Only every now and again did his thoughts lose themselves in a half-sleep of benevolent melancholy. That happened whenever he thought of the secret cult devoted to the originals of the writings before him, and the miracles that had issued from them and moved thousands of people. And those people, because of the great distance separating him from them, now appeared to him as brothers, while he despised those who surrounded him, and whom he saw down to their smallest details. At such times he became ill-tempered. He was oppressed by the thought that his life was condemned to run its course far from the wellsprings of the holy powers, his efforts condemned perhaps to wane through adverse conditions. But when he had spent a while sitting sadly over his books, a strange thing happened to his mood. His melancholy lost nothing of its heaviness; on the contrary, its sadness intensified, but it no longer oppressed him. He felt more forlorn and isolated than ever, but in his melancholy there was a refined pleasure, a pride in doing something strange, serving a deity that no one understood. And then, even fleetingly, something might gleam in his eyes that recalled the madness of religious ecstasy.

Beineberg had talked himself out. The image of his eccentric father lived on in him in a kind of distorting enlargement. Each trait was preserved; but what might originally have been merely a mood in his father, one that was nurtured and intensified for the sake of its exclusiveness, had burgeoned in his son into a fantastic hope. His father's peculiarity, which might originally have meant only the last refuge of his individuality, which each of us must create for himself even if only in his choice of clothes, so as to have something that distinguishes him from others, had, in his son, become a firm conviction that he could achieve domination through unusual spiritual powers.

Törless was familiar enough with these conversations. They passed him by and barely touched him.

He had now half turned away from the window and was studying Beineberg, who was rolling himself a cigarette. And again he felt that curious disgust for Beineberg that sometimes surged up within him. But those slender, dark hands, which were skilfully rolling the tobacco in the paper, were actually beautiful. Thin fingers, oval, beautifully arched nails: there was a certain elegance to them. And in the dark brown eyes. And there was elegance, too, in the elongated slenderness of the boy's whole body. Of course – his ears did stick out a great deal, his face was small and irregular, and the overall impression of his head was like a bat's. However – and Törless felt this very clearly as he weighed up the details against each other – it was not the ugly details so much as the more attractive ones that unsettled him so peculiarly.

The gauntness of his body – Beineberg himself was forever praising the steely, slim legs of Homeric athletes which he took as his model. Törless had not yet made up his mind about this, and no satisfactory comparison occurred to him now. He wanted to stare keenly at Beineberg, but Beineberg would have noticed, and he would have had to start some conversation or other. But precisely in that way – only half looking at him and half completing the picture in his imagination – the difference struck him. If he imagined the clothes away from Beineberg's body, it was almost impossible to maintain the idea of a tranquil slenderness; instead images momentarily came to him of twisting movements, a distortion of the limbs and contortion of the spine, such as one sees in all representations of martyrdom or in the grotesque displays of fairground artistes.

Beineberg's hands, too, which he could equally well have visualized in some shapely gesture, he could only imagine in a fiddling agitation. And it was upon those hands, actually the most beautiful thing about Beineberg, that his greatest disgust was focused. There was something indecent about them. That was probably the right word. And there was also something indecent in the impression of dislocation that his body produced. In a sense it only appeared to collect in his hands, and it seemed to radiate from them like the presentiment of a touch, which sent a twinge of nausea over Törless's skin. He himself was amazed by this idea, and a little shocked. Because this was the second time that day that something sexual had forced its way, unsuspected and without any real relevance, between his thoughts.

Beineberg had picked up a newspaper, and Törless was now able to take a good look at him.

In fact he could hardly find anything that might have served even partly as an excuse for the sudden appearance of such a stream of thoughts.

And yet his discomfort, unfounded though it was, became increasingly vivid. Not ten minutes of silence had passed between the two of them, and yet Törless felt that his disgust had already intensified to an extreme. It seemed for the first time to express an underlying mood, an underlying relationship between himself and Beineberg; a suspicion which had always been present, lying in wait, seemed all of a sudden to have risen to the surface and become a conscious sensation.

The situation between them became ever more intense. Insults for which he knew no words sprang into Törless's mind. He was unsettled by a kind of shame, as though something had actually happened between him and Beineberg. His fingers began to drum uneasily on the tabletop.

Finally, to rid himself of that strange state of mind, he looked out of the window again.

Now Beineberg looked up from the newspaper; then he read out some passage or other, set the paper aside and yawned.

Once the silence was broken, the compulsion that had been

weighing upon Törless was broken as well. Now casual words swept that moment away and erased it. It had been a sudden moment of alertness, which now made way for the old indifference . . .

'How much time do we have left?' asked Törless.

'Two and a half hours.'

Then, with a shiver, he hunched his shoulders. Once again he felt the paralysing force of the confinement that awaited him. The timetable, daily association with his friends. Even that disgust for Beineberg, which seemed for a moment to have created a new situation, would cease to be.

'. . . What's for dinner tonight?'

'I don't know.'

'What subjects do we have tomorrow?'

'Maths.'

'Oh? Did we have any homework?'

'Yes, a few new theorems in trigonometry; but you'll manage, they're nothing special.'

'And then?'

'Divinity.'

'Divinity? Oh yes. That's going to be interesting again . . . When I get into my stride I think I could just as easily prove that twice two is five as that there can be only one God . . .'

Beineberg looked mockingly up at Törless. 'You're really funny about that; it almost seems to me that it even gives you pleasure. Anyway, there's a flash of eagerness shining in your eyes –'

'Why not? Isn't it great? There always comes a point where you don't know whether you're lying, or whether what you've invented is more truthful than you are yourself.'

'How's that?'

'Well, I don't really mean it literally. Of course you always know when you're fibbing; but at the same time what you're saying strikes you as so believable that in a sense you're standing still, imprisoned by your own thoughts.'

'Yes, but what is it that gives you pleasure?'

'Just this. Something like a jolt runs through your head, dizziness, shock – '

'Oh come on, that's so much nonsense.'

'I didn't say it wasn't. But for me at least it's the most interesting thing in the whole school.'

'It's like a way of doing gymnastics with your brain; but there's no real point to it.'

'No,' said Törless, and looked back out into the garden. Behind him – in the distance – he heard the gas flames humming. He pursued a feeling that was rising up in him, mournfully, like a mist.

'There's no point to it. You're right. But you shouldn't say that. All the things we do all day long in school – what of any of it has a point? What do we get from any of it? I mean, anything for ourselves – do you see what I mean? In the evening you know you've been through another day, that you've learned so and so much, you've fulfilled your timetable, but you've remained empty – inside, I mean, you have what you might call an inner hunger . . .'

Beineberg growled something about exercise, preparing one's mind – can't do much about it yet – later . . .

'Preparing? Exercise? What for? Do you know something special? Perhaps you're hoping for something, it's very vague to you as well. This is what it's like: waiting eternally for something and the only thing you know about it is that you're waiting for it . . . That's so boring . . .'

'Boring . . .' Beineberg drawled in imitation, and swayed his head from side to side.

Törless was still looking into the garden. He thought he could hear the rustling of the faded leaves thrown together by the wind. Then came that moment of the most intense silence that always arrives shortly before complete darkness. The forms that had embedded themselves ever deeper in the dusk, and the fading colours, seemed to stand still for seconds at a time, to hold their breath . . .

'Listen, Beineberg,' said Törless, without turning around, 'there are always a few moments at dusk that are unlike anything else. However often I observe it, the same memory returns to me. It was once when I was very small, in the woods, at this time of day. The nursemaid had wandered off; I didn't know, and thought I could still sense her nearby. Suddenly something forced me to look up. I felt I was alone. It was suddenly so still. And when I looked around, it was as though the trees were standing silent in a circle, watching me. I cried; I felt so abandoned by the grown-ups, at the mercy of inanimate beings ... What is that? It often comes back to me. What is that sudden silence that is like a language we can't hear?'

'I'm not familiar with what you're talking about; but why shouldn't objects have a language? We can't even claim with any certainty that they don't have a soul!'

Törless didn't reply. He felt ill at ease with Beineberg's speculative vision of things.

After a while, however, Beineberg began: 'Why do you keep looking through the window? What's out there?'

'I'm still thinking about what it might have been.' But in reality he was already thinking about something else, something that he didn't want to admit. The great tension, the act of listening in to a solemn mystery, and the responsibility of gazing into still unfathomed relationships between things, was something that he had been able to bear only for a moment. Then that feeling of being alone and abandoned, which always followed that excessive exertion, enveloped him once again. He felt: there's something in this that is still too hard for me, and his thoughts fled to something else that was also part of it, but to a certain extent only in the background, lying in wait: loneliness.

From the deserted garden a leaf danced every now and again to the illuminated window, cutting a bright strip into the darkness, which seemed to shrink back to avoid it, then to step forward again a moment later and stand motionless like a wall outside the windows. It was a world all to itself, the darkness. Like a black enemy horde it had fallen across the earth and killed the people or driven them out or done whatever it had done to make sure that it erased every last trace of them.

And Törless felt as though he was pleased. At that moment he did not like people, grown-ups, adults. He never liked them when it was dark. Then, he was used to imagining people away. When he had done that, the world appeared to him as a gloomy, deserted house, and a shudder ran through his breast, as though he had now to look from room to room – dark rooms, with who knows what hidden in their corners – tentatively stepping across the thresholds that no man's foot but his would walk upon – and in one room the doors would suddenly fall open in front of him and behind him and he would stand face to face with the mistress of the black hordes. And at that moment the locks of all the doors he had passed through would also fall shut, and only far outside the walls would the shadows of darkness stand guard like black eunuchs, keeping human beings at bay.

That was his kind of loneliness, since being left on his own that time – in the wood, where he had wept so. It held for him the charm of a woman and of something monstrous. He felt that it was like a woman, but her breath was only a choking in his breast, her face a whirling oblivion of all human faces and the movements of her hands shudders running over his body . . .

He was afraid of that fantasy, because he was aware of its lascivious furtiveness, and he was unsettled at the thought that such ideas might win ever greater mastery over him. But they overwhelmed him precisely when he imagined himself at his most serious and pure. As a reaction, it might be said, to the moments when he became aware of emotional realizations which were preparing themselves within him, but which were not yet appropriate to his age. For early in the development of every fine moral force there is such a point, when the soul weakens, and that will perhaps be its boldest moment – as though it must first put down searching roots in order to churn up the earth destined later to support it –

which is why adolescent boys with great futures ahead of them possess a past rich in humiliations.

Törless's love of particular moods was the first sign of a spiritual development that would later express itself as a talent for astonishment. Later, in fact, he was practically controlled by a peculiar ability. He was often forced to feel events, people, things, even himself, in such a way that he had a sense both of some mystery that could not be solved, and of some inexplicable affinity that could never quite be justified. They seemed palpably within reach of his understanding, and yet could never entirely be broken down into words and thoughts. Between events and himself, indeed, between his own emotions and some innermost self which craved that they be understood, there always remained a dividing line which retreated like a horizon from his yearning the closer he came to it. Indeed, the more precisely he circumscribed his sensations with his thoughts, the more familiar they became to him, the stranger and more incomprehensible he felt them to be, so that it no longer even seemed as though they were retreating from him and more as though he himself was moving away from them, while remaining unable to shake off the notion that he was coming closer to them.

That curious contradiction, so difficult to penetrate, later occupied a considerable phase of his mental development; it seemed to want to tear his soul apart, and for a long time it continued to threaten it, remaining its chief problem.

For the time being, however, the gravity of these struggles was manifest only as a frequent and sudden fatigue, which frightened Törless from a distance as soon as he sensed it – as he had done just now – through some strange, dubious mood. Then he felt himself to be as powerless as an abandoned prisoner, someone closed off equally from himself and from others. He could have screamed with emptiness and despair, but instead he turned away from the serious and expectant, tormented and exhausted person within himself and listened – still frightened by that sudden renunciation and already delighted by its warm, sinful breath – to the whispering voices of his loneliness.

Törless suddenly suggested they pay the bill. There was a flash of understanding in Beineberg's eyes; he knew that mood. Törless was not pleased by this agreement between them; his dislike of Beineberg sprang to life again, and he felt ashamed at what he had in common with him.

But that was almost part of it. Shame is yet another loneliness, a new dark wall.

And without exchanging a word they set off on a particular path.

There must have been a shower of rain a few minutes earlier – the air was moist and heavy, a bright mist trembled around the streetlights, and here and there the pavements glistened.

Törless's sword was striking the cobbles, so he drew it close to his side, but even the sound of his clattering heels made him shiver strangely.

After a while they had soft ground beneath their feet. They left the centre of the town and walked along wide village streets towards the river.

Black and sluggish, the river surged beneath the wooden bridge, making deep gurgling sounds. A single streetlight stood by it, with dusty and broken panes. Its beam, cowering nervously from the gusts of wind, occasionally fell upon a surging wave and flowed away on its back. The rounded planks of the bridge yielded beneath each step . . . rolled forward and back again.

Beineberg stopped. The opposite bank was densely planted with trees which, since the road turned off at right angles and led along the water, looked like a menacing, black, impenetrable wall. Only after careful searching did one find a narrow, hidden path leading straight into the wood. With each step they took, a shower of droplets fell from the dense, lush undergrowth as their clothes brushed past. After a while they had to stop again and light a match.

It was quite still, and even the gurgling of the river could no longer be heard. Suddenly, from far away, an indistinct, broken sound reached them. It sounded like a cry or a warning. Or like the call of some incomprehensible creature crashing through the bushes like themselves. They walked towards the sound, stopped, walked on again. It was perhaps a quarter of an hour altogether before they were relieved to make out loud voices and the sounds of an accordion.

The wood became sparser, and a few paces further on they were standing at the edge of a clearing, with a massive square, two-storey building set in the middle of it.

It was the old bath-house. Used in its day by the citizens of the little town and the peasants of the surrounding area as a spa, it had been almost empty for years. Only in its ground floor there was a disreputable inn.

The two boys stood still for a moment, listening.

Törless was about to step forward out of the bushes, when heavy boots clattered on the steps of the hall and a drunk man tottered uncertainly into the open. Behind him, in the shadow of the hallway, stood a woman, who could be heard whispering something in a hurried, angry voice as though demanding something from him. The man laughed and swayed on his feet. Then they heard what sounded like pleading, but they couldn't make that out either. They could only discern the wheedling, cajoling tone of her voice. Now the woman came further outside and put a hand on the man's shoulder. The moon illuminated her – her petticoat, her jacket, her pleading smile. The man looked straight in front of him, shook his head and kept his hands firmly in his pockets. Then he spat and pushed the woman away, perhaps because she had said something else. Now their voices were louder, and it was possible to hear what they were saying.

'So you're not going to give me anything? You . . . !'

'Just get up there, you filthy slut!'

'Cheek! Coming from a peasant like you!'

By way of reply the drunk clumsily picked up a stone. 'If you don't clear off this minute, I'll give you a good hiding!' and he prepared to throw it. Törless heard the woman making off up the stairs.

The man stood there for a while, indecisively holding the stone. He laughed; looked towards the sky, where the moon swam, wine-yellow between black clouds; then he stared at the dark under-growth of the bushes, as though he was considering heading in that direction. Törless carefully drew back his foot; he could feel his heart beating in his throat. Finally the drunk seemed to have thought better of it. He dropped the stone. With a coarse, trium-phant laugh he yelled a raucous obscenity up at the window, then slipped around the corner.

The two boys didn't move. 'Did you recognize her?' whispered Beineberg; 'It was Božena.' Törless didn't reply; he was listening to hear whether the drunk was coming back again. Then Beineberg pushed him forwards. They jumped quickly and carefully, dodging the light that fell in a wedge through the ground-floor windows, and they found themselves in the dark hallway of the house. A flight of wooden stairs led in narrow bends to the first floor. Here someone must have heard their steps on the clattering stairs, or their swords striking the woodwork – the door of the taproom was opened and someone came to check who was in the building, while the accordion suddenly fell silent and the hubbub of voices paused expectantly for a moment.

Startled, Törless pressed himself against the bend in the stairs, but he must have been seen in spite of the darkness, for he heard the barmaid's mocking voice as the door was being closed, followed by yells of laughter.

The first-floor landing was in total darkness. Neither Törless nor Beineberg dared take a step forward, worried that they might knock something over and make a noise. In their excitement, their fingers fumbled hastily for the doorknob.

*

Božena had come as a peasant girl to the capital, where she went into service and later became a lady's maid.

Everything had gone quite well for her at first. Her peasant manner, which she had not lost, any more than she had lost her broad, solid walk, assured her of the trust of her mistresses, who liked her cow-byre smell for its simplicity, and the amorous attentions of her masters, who liked it for its perfume. Perhaps out of caprice, or perhaps out of discontent and a vague longing for passion, she relinquished that comfortable life. She became a waitress, was taken sick, found lodging in an elegant house of ill repute and, as time passed and her dissolute life wore her down, found herself washed further and further out into the provinces.

Here, finally, where she had now lived for several years, not far from her home village, she helped in the inn by day and in the evening she read cheap novels, smoked cigarettes and received occasional visits from men.

She had not yet become ugly, exactly, but her face was strikingly free of charm, and she clearly made a special effort to stress this even more with her manner. She liked to show that she was very familiar with the elegance and manners of polite society, but was now beyond all that. She liked to say that she cared not a whit for it, as she cared nothing for herself, or for anything at all. For that reason, in spite of her degeneracy, she enjoyed a certain respect among the peasant boys of the area. Certainly, they spat when they spoke of her, and felt obliged to be coarse in their treatment of her, even more so than they were with other girls, but at root they were also very proud of that 'damned whore' who had emerged from their midst and seen so clearly through the world's veneer. They came to see her – one by one, and on the sly, but time and again. This fact brought Božena a residue of pride and justification in her life. She took perhaps even greater satisfaction, though, in her visits from the young gentlemen from the institute. It was for them that she deliberately displayed her crudest and most ugly qualities, because – as she liked to put it – they would come crawling to her anyway.

When the two friends came in, she was lying on her bed as usual, smoking and reading.

Törless, still standing in the doorway, greedily devoured the image of her with his eyes.

'My goodness, what dear little boys have we here?' she cried mockingly as they came in, studying them with some contempt. 'Eh, Baron? What'll Mama have to say about this?' The welcome was typical of her.

'That's enough . . . !' mumbled Beineberg and sat down beside her on the bed. Törless sat down further away; he was irritated because Božena was paying him no attention and acting as though she didn't know him.

Visits to this woman had recently become his sole, secret pleasure. Towards the end of the week he would become restless, and couldn't wait for Sunday when he crept to see her in the evening. His chief preoccupation was the fact that he had to creep in. What would have happened, for example, if it had occurred to the young drunk in the taproom just now to come after him? Just for the sake of giving the depraved young gentleman something to think about? He was no coward, but he knew that he was defenceless here. His dainty sword was a joke compared to those rough fists. And then there was the shame and punishment that he could expect! His only options would be either to run or to beg for mercy. Or ask Božena to protect him. The thought made him shiver. But that was it! Just that! Nothing else! That fear, that abandonment of himself lured him afresh each time. Stepping out of a privileged position to be among the common people; among them – no, lower than them!

He was not depraved. When it came down to it, what predominated was his repugnance at the act, and anxiety about the possible consequences. It was only his imagination that had been taken in an unhealthy direction. When the days of the week laid themselves leadenly over his life, one by one, those caustic enticements began to tempt him. A peculiar seduction formed out of the memories of his visits. Božena appeared to him as a creature of incredible degradation, and his relationship with her, the sensations that he had to undergo, seemed like a cruel cult of self-sacrifice. It thrilled him to have to leave behind everything that normally enclosed him, his privileged position, the thoughts and feelings inculcated in him, everything that gave him nothing and oppressed him. It thrilled him to flee, naked, stripped of everything, racing madly to that woman.

This was much the same as it is with young people in general. If Božena had been pure and beautiful, and if he had been capable of love in those days, he might have bitten her, heightening both her lust and his own to the point of pain. For the first passion of the adolescent boy is not love of one, but hatred for all. That sense of being misunderstood, of not understanding the world, not only goes hand in hand with the first passion, but is also its only non-arbitrary cause. And it too is a form of flight, in which two people's togetherness means only the duplication of their solitude.

Almost every first passion lasts only a short while and leaves a bitter aftertaste. It is a mistake, a disappointment. Afterwards one doesn't understand oneself, and doesn't know whom to blame. This is because the relationships between the protagonists in this drama are largely arbitrary: they are chance companions in flight. Once things have calmed down they no longer recognize one another. They become aware of oppositions between themselves, because they are no longer aware of what they have in common.

The only reason that things were different for Törless was that he was alone. The ageing, degraded prostitute was unable to release all the forces within him. But she was woman enough to draw parts of his innermost being, waiting like ripening grains for the fertilizing moment, prematurely to the surface.

These were, then, his strange ideas and fantastic temptations. But sometimes he felt equally close to throwing himself on the ground and screaming with despair.

*

Božena was still not paying any attention to Törless. She seemed to be doing it out of spite, just to annoy him. Suddenly she interrupted her conversation: 'Give me some money, I'll get some tea and schnapps.'

Törless gave her one of the silver coins he had received from his mother that afternoon.

She fetched a battered spirit-lamp from the window-sill and lit the paraffin; then shuffled slowly down the stairs.

Beineberg gave Törless a nudge. 'Why are you being so pathetic? She'll think you don't dare.'

'Leave me out of it,' said Törless, 'I don't feel like it. Just go on talking to her. Why is she forever going on about your mother?'

'Ever since she's learned my name she claims she was once in service with my aunt and knew my mother. Part of it seems to be true, but partly she's certainly lying – just for the hell of it; although I don't understand what's so funny about it.'

Törless blushed; a strange thought had occurred to him. But then Božena returned with the schnapps and sat back down on the bed beside Beineberg. And she immediately resumed their earlier conversation.

'. . . Yes, your mama was a beautiful girl. You don't look at all like her, with your sticking-out ears. She was a merry one, too. She'll have turned a few heads, I'm sure. And quite right, too.'

After a pause something particularly amusing seemed to have occurred to her: 'Your uncle, the officer in the dragoons, you remember? Karl I think his name was, he was a cousin of your mother's, how he used to court her in those days! But on Sunday, when the ladies were at church, I was the one he'd come after. Every few minutes I'd have to bring something else to his room. He was smartly dressed, I remember that, but he had a nerve . . .' She accompanied these words with a telling laugh. Then she expanded on this subject, which apparently gave her especial pleasure. She spoke in an impertinent and familiar way, apparently intent on sullying every word. '. . . I mean, your mother liked him, too. If she'd had any idea what was going on! I think your aunt would have thrown both of us out of the house. That's the way the fine ladies are, especially when they don't have a husband yet. Dear Božena this and dear Božena that – that's how it was all day long. But when the cook was expecting, you should have heard what they had to say! I reckon she thought the likes of us only washed their feet once a year. She said nothing to the cook, but I could hear them talking about it if I happened to be working in the room. Your mother would pull a face as though she wanted to drink nothing but eau-de-Cologne. And not long after that your aunt's belly was up to her nose . . .'

While Božena was talking, Törless felt almost defencelessly exposed to her vulgar insinuations.

He could see what she was describing vividly before him. Beineberg's mother became his own. He remembered the bright rooms of his parents' apartment. The well-groomed, clean, unapproachable faces that had often instilled a certain awe in him during dinner parties at home. The elegant, cool hands, which never seemed to lose any of their dignity, even at dinner. Many such details came into his mind, and he was ashamed to be here in a foul-smelling little room, trembling as he replied to the humiliating words of a whore. The memory of the perfect manners of that society, which never failed to observe the proprieties, had a more powerful effect on him than any moral considerations. His dark, nagging passions struck him as ludicrous. With visionary vividness he saw a cool, dismissive gesture, a shocked smile, like that with which one would shoo away a small and unclean animal. None the less he remained in his seat as though unable to move.

With each remembered detail, shame welled up in him, and with it a series of ugly thoughts. It had begun when Beineberg supplied an explanation of Božena's conversation, and it had made Törless blush.

At that moment he had suddenly found himself thinking of his own mother, and that thought had taken hold of him and would not be shifted. It had just shot through the boundaries of his consciousness – as fast as lightning or too distant to be distinguished – on the edge – as if seen in flight – it could barely be called a thought. And a series of questions had rapidly followed, in an attempt to cover it over: 'How can this Božena compare her vile existence to that of my mother? How can she rub shoulders with her within the confines of a single thought? Why does she not touch her forehead to the ground merely to speak of her? Why is she not forced to admit, as though separated by a great abyss, that they have nothing in common? For what is the true state of affairs? This woman is, for me, a tangle of everything that is sexually desirable; and my mother is a creature who has until now walked through my life at a cloudless distance, clear and without depth, like a star beyond all desire.'

But these questions were not the core of the matter. They barely touched it. They were something secondary; something that had occurred to Törless only in retrospect. They proliferated only because none of them identified the question at hand. They were only excuses, paraphrases of the fact that on the preconscious level, suddenly, instinctively, there was a spiritual connection that had given them all a disagreeable answer. Törless feasted on Božena with his eyes, and at the same time he was unable to forget his mother; the two of them were connected through him: everything else was merely squirming around under that twisted loop of ideas. That was the only fact. But because he was unable to shake off its compulsion, it assumed a terrible, vague significance, which accompanied all his efforts like a perfidious smile.

Törless looked around the room in order to rid his mind of all this. But everything had now absorbed that one relationship. The little iron stove with the rust patches on its plate, the bed with the rickety posts and the headboard with its paint flaking off, the dirty blankets peeping through the holes of the worn cover; Božena, her shift that had slipped from one shoulder, the vulgar, florid scarlet of her petticoat, her broad, cackling laugh; finally Beineberg, whose behaviour now, compared with his normal demeanour, seemed like that of a depraved priest who has lost his reason and weaves innuendoes into the solemn forms of a prayer . . . everything headed in a single direction, invaded him and twisted his thoughts violently back again and again.

Only in one place did his eyes, which fled in terror from Božena to Beineberg, find peace. That was above the little curtain. There the clouds looked in from the sky, and, motionless, the moon.

It was as though he had suddenly stepped out into the fresh, peaceful night air. For a while all his thoughts grew quite still. Then a pleasant memory came to him. The house in the country where they had spent the previous summer. Nights in the silent park. A velvet-dark firmament quivering with stars. His mother's voice from the depths of the garden, where she was walking with Papa on the faintly shimmering gravel paths. Songs that she sang quietly to herself. But again . . . a cold shiver ran through him . . . there was that painful comparison. What might the two of them have been feeling? Love? No, the idea was now occurring to him for the first time. Love was something quite different. Not something for grown-ups and adults; let alone for his parents. Sitting by the open window at night and feeling abandoned, feeling different from the grown-ups, feeling misunderstood by every laugh and every mocking look, being unable to explain to anyone what one meant, and longing for someone who might understand . . . that is love! But you have to be young and lonely for that. With them it must have been something else; something peaceful and serene. Mama was simply singing in the evening in the dark garden and being cheerful . . .

But that was precisely what Törless didn't understand. The patient plans with which, for an adult, the days join up into months and years without his so much as noticing, those were still something alien to him. And so was that blunt insensitivity which doesn't even mind that another day is coming to an end. His life was geared towards each new day. Every night was for him a void, a grave, an extinction . . . He had not yet learned the ability to lie down to die each day without a thought.

For that reason he had always suspected that there was something in the background that was being kept from him. Nights seemed to him to be dark portals to mysterious delights which had been kept secret from him, leaving his life empty and sad.

He remembered something he had observed on one of those evenings – a peculiar laugh of his mother's as she pressed herself, as if joking, closer to her husband's arm. It seemed to rule out any doubt. And there must be a door leading here from the world of those calm and unimpeachable people. And now that he knew he could only think about it with that particular smile, expressing a malicious mistrust that he tried in vain to resist . . .

In the meantime Božena went on talking. Törless listened half attentively. She was talking about someone else who came almost every Sunday . . . 'What can his name be? He's in your year.'

'Reiting?'

'No.'

'What does he look like?'

'He's about the same height as that one there,' Božena pointed to Törless, 'but his head's a bit too big.'

'Ah, Basini?'

'Yes, yes, that's what he called himself. He's very odd. And very classy; he only drinks wine. But he's thick. It costs him a lot of money, and all he ever does is tell me stories. He goes on about the love affairs he claims he has at home; what good does that do him? I can tell this is the first time in his life that he's been with a woman. You're just a boy, too, but you're cheeky; but he's awkward and nervous, and that's why he talks on and on at me about how you've got to treat women if you're a sensualist – that's the word he uses. He says it's all women are fit for; what would you lot know about that?'

Beineberg gave her a mocking grin in reply.

'Just you laugh!' Božena barked at him, amused, 'I once asked him if he wouldn't be ashamed if his mother could see him. "Mother? . . . Mother? . . ." he said. "What's that? There's no such thing, now. I left all that at home before I came to see you . . ." That's right, just you listen, that's what you're like! Nice little sons you are, you fine young gentlemen; I could almost feel sorry for your mothers! . . .'

At these words Törless remembered his earlier notion of himself. Leaving everything behind him and betraying the image of his parents. And now he was forced to see that he wasn't even doing something terribly solitary, just something quite vulgar. He was ashamed. But the other thoughts were there again as well. They're doing it too! They're betraying you! You have secret associates! Maybe it's different for them in some way, but in essence it must still be the same: a mysterious, terrible joy. Something in which one can drown oneself along with all one's fear of the monotony of days . . . Might they even know something more? Something quite out of the ordinary? Because they're so calm during the day . . . and that laugh of your mother's? As though she was calmly walking to close all the doors . . .

In the midst of this argument there came a moment at which Törless abandoned himself and yielded, heart choking, to the storm.

And at that very moment Božena rose to her feet and walked over to him.

'Why isn't the little one saying anything? Is he worried about something?'

Beineberg whispered something and smiled maliciously.

'What, homesick are we? Has Mummy gone and left him? And the nasty boy comes running straight to someone like me!'

Božena tenderly buried her hand in his hair, fingers splayed. 'Go on, don't be stupid. Give me a kiss, there. The nobility aren't made of sugar-candy,' and she bent his head back.

Törless wanted to say something, to stir himself to make a crude joke. He felt that everything now depended upon saying something irrelevant, but he couldn't utter a sound. With a petrified smile he stared into the ravaged face above his own, into those vacant eyes, then the outside world began to grow smaller . . . to move further and further away . . . For a moment the image of that peasant lad who had picked up the stone came into his mind and seemed to scoff at him . . . then he was quite alone.

'Hey, I've got him,' whispered Reiting.

'Who?'

'The locker thief.'

Törless had just come back with Beineberg. It was just before supper-time, and the staff on duty had already gone home. Chattering groups had formed among the green tables, and a warm life hummed and whirred through the hall.

It was an ordinary classroom with whitewashed walls, a big black crucifix and portraits of the Emperor and Empress on either side of the blackboard. Next to the big iron stove, as yet unlit, some of them on the podium, some on chairs arranged around it, sat the young people who had accompanied Herr and Frau Törless to the station that afternoon. Apart from Reiting, they were tall Hofmeier and Jusch, the nickname given to a little Polish count.

Törless was fairly curious.

The lockers were at the back of the classroom, long boxes with lockable drawers, in which the pupils at the institute stored their letters, books, money and every imaginable knick-knack.

And for some time a number of individuals had been complaining that they were missing small sums of money, although they were unable to voice specific suspicions.

Beineberg was the first to be able to say with certainty that – the previous week – a large sum had been stolen. But only Reiting and Törless knew about it.

They suspected the servants.

'Go on, tell us!' asked Törless, but Reiting gestured quickly at him.

'Psst! Later. No one knows anything about it.'

'A servant?' whispered Törless.

'No.'

'So can you at least give us a hint who it is?'

Reiting turned away from the others and said quietly, 'B.' No one but Törless had understood any of this hushed conversation, but it leaped out at him like an ambush. B.? – it could only be Basini. And that couldn't be! His mother was a wealthy lady, he was addressed as Excellency. Törless couldn't believe it, and the thought of Božena's story came to mind.

He could hardly wait for the moment when the others went for their meal. Beineberg and Reiting stayed behind, claiming still to be full from lunchtime.

Reiting suggested that they should 'go upstairs' first.

They stepped out into the corridor, which stretched endlessly outside the classroom. The flickering gas flames illuminated it only for brief stretches, and footsteps echoed from one niche to the next, however quietly one walked . . .

Perhaps fifty metres away from the door a flight of steps led to the second floor, which housed the nature cabinet, other collections of educational material and a large number of empty rooms.

From that point onwards the stairs grew narrow and rose, in a series of short landings running into one another at right angles, to the attic. And – as old buildings are often constructed illogically, with an excess of corners and steps leading nowhere – they led some distance further beyond the level of the attic, so that one had to take a flight of wooden steps beyond the heavy locked iron door to get down to it.

But on this side a lost room was created, several metres high, which reached up to the roof beams. This room, where no one ever set foot, had been used to store old stage sets from performances that no one could remember.

Even on bright afternoons the daylight on the stairs was suffocated in a gloom choked with old dust, because this approach to the attic, facing towards the wing of the massive building, was hardly ever used.

From the last step of the stairs Beineberg swung over the banisters and lowered himself down between the stage sets, holding on to the posts. Reiting and Törless did likewise. There they were able to find a solid footing on a crate that had been put there for that purpose, and from there they leaped to land on the floor.

Even if the eyes of someone standing on the stairs had grown accustomed to the dark, he would have been unable to distinguish anything other than a motionless confusion of jagged stage sets, variously shoved into one another.

But when Beineberg pushed one of them slightly aside, a narrow, tube-like passageway opened up to the boys standing below.

They hid the crate that had helped them in climbing down, and pushed their way between the stage sets.

Here it became completely dark, and one would have needed a very precise knowledge of the place in order to find one's way forward. Every now and again one of the big canvas walls rustled as someone brushed past it, and there was the scurrying sound of startled mice, and a mildewed smell of forgotten trunks.

The three boys, who knew this way well, felt their way forward, extremely carefully, taking care with each step they took not to bump into one of the strings stretched across the floor as a trap and alarm.

After a while they reached a small door on the right, just before the wall that separated off the attic.

When Beineberg opened it, they found themselves in a narrow space below the top landing, which, in the light of a small, flickering oil-lamp that Beineberg had lit, looked quite bizarre.

The ceiling was only horizontal where it ran directly beneath the landing, and even there it was only just high enough for a person to stand upright. But it sloped away towards the rear, following the outline of the stairs, finishing up in an acute angle. At the opposite side of the room a thin partition wall divided the attic from the stairwell, and its third wall was naturally formed by the masonry supporting the staircase. Only the second side wall, into which the door was set, seemed to have been added specially. It seemed to owe its existence to the intention of creating a little storeroom for implements here, or perhaps it was even down to a whim of the architect, who might, at the sight of this dark corner, have had the medieval notion of walling it up into a hiding place.

At any rate, apart from the three boys, no one in the whole school knew of the existence of this room, let alone bothering to assign it a purpose.

So the boys were able to deck it out according to their own bizarre purposes.

The walls were lined with a blood-red canvas, which Reiting and Beineberg had purloined from one of the attic rooms, and the floor was covered with a double layer of a thick, woolly fabric, like the material used as second blankets in the dormitories in winter. In the front part of the store room stood narrow little fabric-covered boxes, which were used as seats; at the back, where floor and ceiling ended up in the sharp corner, a sleeping place had been arranged. It provided a bed for three to four people, which could be darkened by a curtain and separated off from the front part of the storeroom.

On the wall beside the door hung a loaded revolver.

Törless didn't like the storeroom. He did, though, like the confinement of it, the solitude, like being deep in the interior of a mountain, and the smell of the dusty old stage sets filled him with vague sensations. But the concealment, the alarm cord, the revolver, which were supposed to give an extreme illusion of defiance and furtiveness, all struck him as ridiculous. It was as though the boys were trying to convince themselves they were leading the lives of bandits.

In fact, Törless was only joining in because he didn't want to lag behind the others. But Beineberg and Reiting took these things terribly seriously. Törless was aware of that. He knew that Beineberg owned copies of the keys to all the cellars and attic rooms in the school. He knew that Beineberg often vanished from class for hours at a time, to sit somewhere – high up in the beams of the attic or beneath the ground in one of the many branching, crumbling vaults – and read adventure stories by the light of a little lantern that he always carried with him, or think thoughts about supernatural matters.

He knew something similar about Reiting. He too had his hidden corner, where he kept secret diaries; but these were filled with deranged plans for the future, and with precise notes about the cause, staging and development of the many intrigues that he instigated among his classmates. For Reiting knew no greater pleasure than setting people against one another, defeating one with the help of the other. He revelled in extorted favours and flattery, feeling the resentment of hatred behind the mask.

'It's just an exercise,' was his only excuse, and he delivered it with a charming laugh. His other form of exercise was to go almost daily to some remote place and box against a wall, a tree or a table, to strengthen his arms and reinforce his hands with calluses.

Törless knew about all of this, but he understood it only up to a point. On a number of occasions he had followed both Reiting and Beineberg on their unconventional journeys. He had indeed taken pleasure in the irregularity of it. And afterwards he also enjoyed walking into the daylight, among the other boys, into the midst of the general merriment, while within him, in his eyes and ears, the stimuli of solitude and the hallucinations of darkness still quivered. But when, on such an occasion, in order to talk to somebody about themselves, Beineberg or Reiting dissected what it was that prompted them to act in such a way, his comprehension failed him. He even found Reiting somewhat hysterical. Reiting liked to talk about the fact that his father had been a curiously unstable person, who had finally gone missing. His name was thought to have been an incognito for that of a very noble family. He believed that his mother would yet tell him of exalted claims to which he was entitled; he dreamed of high politics and *coups d'état*, and consequently wanted to become an officer.

Törless could not seriously imagine such ambitions. The age of revolutions seemed to him to have been consigned to the past once and for all. But Reiting was able to put his ideas into effect, even if it was only on a small scale for the time being. He was a tyrant, and ruthless in his treatment of anyone who resisted him. His allegiances switched from one day to the next, but the majority was always on his side. That was where his talent lay. One or two years previously he had waged a great battle against Beineberg, in which the latter had been defeated. Beineberg had ended up somewhat isolated, despite the fact that in his judgement of people, in his cold-bloodedness and his ability to stir up antipathies towards those he disliked, he was almost a match for his adversary. But he lacked Reiting's affable, winning qualities. His composure and unctuous philosophizing made almost everyone suspicious of him. Unpleasant depravities of some kind were assumed to lie at the root of his nature. But he had caused Reiting great difficulties, and Reiting's victory had come about only by chance. Since then they had made common cause for their mutual benefit.

Törless, on the other hand, remained indifferent to these things. Consequently he was not skilled in them. None the less, he had been included in this world, and each day he could plainly see what it meant to have the most important role in such a state — for in such an institute each class is a little state in itself. For that reason he had a certain timid respect for his two friends. His occasional impulses to copy them went no further than dilettante experiments. As a result, being in any case younger than they were, he became something like a pupil or apprentice to them. He enjoyed their protection, but they were happy to listen to his advice. For Törless had the liveliest mind. Once he had set on a course of action, he was extremely fertile when it came to dreaming up the most evasive combinations. No one was as adept as he at predicting the various possibilities that might be thrown up by a person's behaviour in a particular situation. He failed only when it came to making a decision and, at his own risk, accepting one of the available psychological possibilities as the definite one and acting accordingly; then he lost his interest and had no energy. But he enjoyed his role as a secret chief of staff. All the more so since it was more or less the only one that in any way roused him from his profound internal boredom.

But sometimes he became aware of the cost of this inner dependence. He felt that everything he did was only a game, only something that helped him pass the time of his larval existence at the institute. He felt that it bore no reference to his true nature, which would only come later, at some indefinite point in the future.

When, on certain occasions, he saw how seriously his two friends took these matters, he felt his intellect failing him. He wanted to make fun of them, but was afraid that there was more truth behind their fantasies than he was able to see. In a sense he felt torn between two worlds, one that was solidly respectable, in which everything took place in regular and rational ways, the world to which he was accustomed at home, and a world of adventure, full of darkness, mystery, blood and unimagined surprises. The one seemed to exclude the other. A mocking smile that he would have liked to keep on his lips crossed paths with a shudder running down his spine. His thoughts began to shimmer . . .

It was then that he longed finally to feel something definite within himself; to feel solid needs that were capable of telling good from bad, of distinguishing that which might be used from that which was useless; the ability to make a choice, even if one chose incorrectly – rather than absorbing everything indiscriminately . . .

When he had walked into the room, that dichotomy within him had overwhelmed him once more, as it always did in this place.

Meanwhile Reiting had started to tell his story:

Basini had owed him money, had kept putting him off from one date to the next, always giving his word of honour. 'Up to that point I didn't mind,' said Reiting. 'The longer it went on like that, the more dependent on me he became. After all, a word of honour broken three or four times isn't such a trivial matter, is it? But in the end I needed my money myself. I pointed this out to him, and he swore on his mother's life. Again, of course, he failed to keep his word. Then I told him I would report him. He asked for two days' grace, because he was waiting for a consignment from his guardian. But I did a bit of digging into his circumstances. I wanted to know who else he was dependent on – there's sure to be somebody.

'I didn't much like what I found out. He had debts with Jusch and a few others as well. He had paid part of it back – with the money he owed me, of course. The others were turning the heat on. That annoyed me. Did he think I was a pushover? I wouldn't have liked that, I can tell you. But I thought to myself, "Just wait. There'll be an opportunity to cure him of that little notion." In conversation he had once told me how much money he was expecting, to put my mind at rest that it was greater than my own credit. I asked around, and discovered that the amount fell far short of the total sum of his debts. "Aha," I thought to myself, "now he's going to have another go."

'And sure enough, he came to me, confidentially, and, because the others were giving him a hard time, he asked me for a bit of leniency. But this time I stayed quite cold. "Go and beg from the others," I told him, "I'm not in the habit of taking second place to them." "I know you better, I trust you more," he said. "My final word: either you bring the money tomorrow or I impose my conditions." "What kind of conditions?" he asked. You should have heard him! As though he was prepared to sell his soul. "What kind of conditions? Oho! You have to obey me in whatever I do." "And that's it? Of course I'll do that, I'm happy to stick with you of my own accord." "Oh, not just when it pleases you; you have to do whatever I want – in blind obedience!" Now he squinted at me, half grinning and half embarrassed. He didn't know how far he could take it, how serious I was. He would probably have liked to promise me anything, but he was afraid that I was just putting him to the test. So finally he said with a blush, "I'll bring you the money." I was having fun with him, he was a person I had never really paid any attention to among fifty others. He never really counted, did he? And now, all of a sudden, he had come so close to me that I could see inside him, down to the tiniest detail. I knew for certain that he was prepared to sell himself, without a great deal of fuss, so long as no one knew about it. It was really a surprise, and it's the nicest thing in the world when someone suddenly reveals himself to you like that, and his way of life, to which you've never paid any attention before, is suddenly laid out before you like the worm tunnels when a piece of wood cracks in two . . .

'The next day he actually did bring me the money. More than that, in fact, he invited me to go for a drink with him in the Casino. He ordered wine, cake, cigarettes, and asked me if he could wait on me – out of "gratitude" for all my patience. The only thing I didn't like was that he seemed so terribly innocuous. As if never a hurtful word had ever passed between us. I pointed this out; he only became all the heartier. It was as though he was trying to get out of my clutches, to put himself on an equal footing with me again. He told me nothing more about himself, with every second word he reassured me of our friendship; only something in his eyes clung on to me, as though he was afraid he might be in danger of losing that artificially created sense of intimacy. In the end I found him repellent. I thought, "Does he think I have to put up with this?" and reflected on how I might take the wind out of his sails. I was trying to come up with something really hurtful. I remembered that Beineberg had told me just that morning that he had had some money stolen. It only occurred to me in passing. But it kept coming back. And it really seized me by the throat. "It would be just the right moment," I thought, and casually asked him how much money he had left. I did a quick sum and it added up. "So who was stupid enough to lend you money in spite of everything?" I asked with a laugh. "Hofmeier."

'I must have trembled with joy. Hofmeier had come to me two hours previously to borrow some money for himself. So the idea that had just passed through my head a few minutes before suddenly became a reality. Like when you think to yourself, as a joke: I'd like that house to go on fire right this minute, and a moment later flames shoot yards into the air . . .

'I quickly ran through all the possibilities again; of course I couldn't be sure, but my feeling was enough for me. So I leaned towards him and said in the kindliest way you can imagine, as though I was gently driving a slender, pointed skewer into this brain, "Look here, my dear Basini, why are you lying to me?" As I said that, his eyes seemed to swim in his head with fear, but I went on: "Perhaps you'll be able to pull the wool over somebody's eyes, but not mine. You see, Beineberg . . .' He turned neither red nor white, it was as though he was waiting for a misunderstanding to be cleared up. "Well, to put it briefly," I said, "the money you've used to pay my debt is the money you took last night from Beineberg's drawer!"

'I leaned back to survey the impression. He had turned cherry-red; he choked on his words, his lips flecked with spittle; finally he managed to speak. He came out with a whole torrent of accusations against me: how could I dare to claim any such thing; what could even remotely justify such a fantastical assumption; he said I only wanted a fight with him because he was weaker than I was; that I was only doing it because I was annoyed that he had freed himself from me by paying off his debts; but that he would tell the class . . . the prefects . . . the headmaster; that God could testify to his innocence, and so on *ad infinitum*. I really began to worry that I had done him an injustice and hurt him unnecessarily, he looked so sweet with his red face . . . he looked like a tormented, defenceless little animal. But I couldn't just let it go. So I kept a fixed, mocking smile on my face – almost out of embarrassment – as I listened to everything he was coming out with. Every now and again I nodded and said quietly: "But I know you did it."

'After a while he did calm down. I went on smiling. I had the feeling that I could turn him into the thief just with that smile, even if he hadn't been the one. "And," I thought, "there's plenty of time to put it right."'

'After a few minutes, during which he stole occasional glances at me, he suddenly turned pale. A curious change occurred in his face. It lost its innocent, beautiful charm – it had drained away with the colour. Now it looked greenish, cheesy, swollen. I had only ever seen anything like that once before – when I was walking along the street just as they arrested a murderer. He too had been walking among the other people, and no one could have spotted anything special about him. But when the policeman put his hand on his shoulder, he suddenly became a different person. His face was transformed, and his eyes stared in terror, searching for some kind of escape route; he had the face of a hanged man.

'The change in Basini's expression reminded me of that; I knew everything now, and all I had to do was wait . . .

'And wait I did. I didn't have to say a word, and Basini – exhausted by the silence – began to cry and beg me for mercy. He had only taken the money out of desperation; if I hadn't spotted it, he would have returned it so quickly that no one would have known about it. So I shouldn't say that he'd stolen; he had only borrowed it secretly . . . he couldn't get any further for weeping.

'But then he started pleading once more. He would be obedient to me, do anything I wanted, only I mustn't tell anyone about it. For that price he was practically offering himself to me as a slave, and the mixture of cunning and greedy fear that wriggled into his eyes was disgusting. So I just promised him curtly that I would give some thought to what was going to happen to him, but said that this was primarily a matter for Beineberg. So what, in your opinion, should we do with him?'

While Reiting was talking, Törless had been listening in silence, eyes closed. From time to time he had shivered to his fingertips, and thoughts rose to the surface in his head, as wild and disorganized as bubbles in boiling water. It is said that this is what happens when we have our first glimpse of the woman who will draw us into a devastating passion. It is claimed that there is just such a moment of stooping, of summoning our strength, holding our breath, a moment of outward silence above the greatest internal tension that exists between two human beings. There is no way of saying what takes place in that moment. It is, so to speak, the shadow that passion casts ahead of itself. An organic shadow; a relaxation of all earlier tensions and at the same time a new and sudden state of bondage which contains the whole of the future; an incubation concentrated on the point of a needle . . . And on the other hand it is a nothing, a dull, vague feeling, a weakness, an anxiety . . .

That was how Törless felt. If he thought about it, what Reiting was saying about himself and Basini seemed to him to be of no importance. A thoughtless offence, a cowardly misdeed by Basini, which was sure to be followed by some cruel caprice on the part of Reiting. On the other hand, however, he felt with anxious apprehension that events had now taken a quite personal turn against him, and that there was something in the incident that threatened him, like a sharp-pointed weapon.

He couldn't help imagining Basini at Božena's, and looked around the room. Its walls seemed to threaten him, to sink down upon him, to reach out to him as though with bloody hands, and the revolver rocked back and forth where it hung . . .

Something had dropped for the first time like a stone into the vague loneliness of his daydreams; it was there; there was nothing to be done about it; it was reality. Yesterday Basini had been exactly as he was; a trapdoor had opened, and Basini had fallen. Exactly as Reiting described: a sudden alteration, and the person was someone else . . .

And again that was somehow linked with Božena. His thoughts had blasphemed. He had been confused by a rotten, sweet smell rising from them. And that profound humiliation, that self-abandonment, that state of being covered by the pale, heavy, poisonous leaves of shame that had passed through his dreams like a disembodied, distant reflection, had suddenly become reality for Basini.

So was it something that really had to be reckoned with, something one had to guard against, something that might suddenly leap out of the silent mirrors of thought?

But in that case everything else was possible too. In that case Reiting and Beineberg were possible. This little room was possible ... Then it was also possible that a portal led from the bright, daytime world which had hitherto been the only one he knew, and into another world that was gloomy, surging, passionate, naked, annihilating. That between those whose lives move in an orderly manner from office to family and back, as though in a solid and transparent building of glass and iron, and the others, those who have been cast down, the blood-stained, the debauched and the filthy, who wander a confusion of passageways echoing with roaring voices, there is not a bridge, but it is rather that their boundaries abut, secret and close, and ready to be crossed at any moment ...

And one question alone remains: how is it possible? What happens in such moments? What shoots screaming into the air, what is suddenly extinguished?

Those were the questions that this event brought to Törless's mind. They rose up indistinctly, lips sealed, disguised by a dull, vague feeling ... a weakness, an anxiety.

But some of their words echoed in Törless as though from afar, scrappy and random, and filled him with anxious foreboding.

Reiting's question came at that moment.

Straight away Törless began to speak. He was obeying a sudden urge, a feeling of dismay. It seemed to him that something crucial was about to happen, and he was afraid of that approaching event, he wanted to avoid it, to gain some grace ... He spoke, but immediately he felt that he had nothing relevant to say, that his words had no inner substance and were not his true opinion ...

He said, 'Basini is a thief.' And the hard, definite sound of the word made him feel so good that he repeated it twice. '... a thief. And thieves are punished – everywhere, throughout the whole world. He must be reported, removed from the institute! Let him mend his ways somewhere else, he's no longer one of us!'

But Reiting said with a look of unpleasant consternation: 'No, why should we take it to the limit straight away?'

'Why? Don't you think it's obvious?'

'Far from it. You're acting as though the fire and brimstone were just around the corner, ready to engulf us all if we kept Basini among us for a moment longer. Things aren't as bad as all that.'

'How can you say that? Here you've got someone who's stolen, who's then offered himself to you as a maid, as a slave, and you're telling me you're going to go on from day to day sitting down with him, eating with him, sleeping with him? I can't understand that. After all, we're being educated together because we belong to the same society. Wouldn't you care if you were eventually to find yourself standing next to him in your regiment, or working in the same ministry, if he were to socialize with the same families as you – if he were even to court your own sister –?'

'Come on, you're exaggerating now!' laughed Reiting. 'You're acting as though we belong to a lifelong brotherhood. Do you think we're always going to bear a seal around our necks: "Educated at the Seminary in W. Bears certain privileges and obligations"? Later on, each one of us is going to go his own way, and each of us will become whatever it is that he's qualified to do, because it isn't as though there's just a single society. So I don't think we should concern ourselves too much about the future. And where the present is concerned, I think I said that we should remain classmates with Basini. We'll find some way of ensuring that there's a distance between us. We're holding Basini in the palm of our hands, we can do whatever we like with him, you can spit at him twice a day as far as I'm concerned: as long as he puts up with that, what do we have in common with him? And if he refuses, we can still show him who's in charge ... You just have to drop the idea that anything connects us with Basini apart from the pleasure we get from the fact that he's vile!'

Although Törless wasn't at all convinced of his case, he eagerly continued: 'Listen, Reiting, why are you so keen on taking Basini's side?'

'Am I taking his side? I really don't know. I have no special reason to; the whole business leaves me completely indifferent. I'm just annoyed by your exaggeration. What's got into you? That kind of idealism, I mean. Holy enthusiasm for the school or for justice. You have no idea how tired and hackneyed it sounds. Either that or,' and Reiting winked suspiciously over at Törless, 'might you have some other reason why Basini should be thrown out and you just don't want to show your colours? Some old revenge? Then tell us! Because if it's good enough we might be able to make use of it.'

Törless turned to Beineberg, who merely grinned. Between utterances he drew on a long chibouk, sitting with his legs crossed in the oriental style, and, with his ears sticking out in the murky light, he resembled the grotesque figure of an idol. 'You can do whatever you like as far as I'm concerned; I don't care about the money, or about justice. In India they would drive a pointed bamboo through his guts; at least that would be fun. He's stupid and cowardly, there's nothing else wrong with him, and as long as I live I really couldn't care what happens to people like that. They themselves are nothing, and we don't know what's going to happen to their souls. May Allah bestow his mercy on your judgement!'

Törless made no reply. After Reiting had contradicted him and Beineberg had refused to take sides, he had finished. He could manage no further resistance; he felt he no longer had any desire to stop the unknown event on the horizon.

So Reiting made a suggestion, which they accepted. They decided to keep Basini under surveillance for the time being, in a sense to become his guardians, and thus present him with an opportunity to extricate himself. His income and spending would be rigorously scrutinized, and his relations with the other boys would be contingent on the permission of the three.

This decision seemed to be quite correct and benevolent. This time Reiting didn't describe it as 'hackneyed and insipid'. Because although they didn't admit it, they each felt that this should be only a kind of interim state. Reiting had been unhappy about passing up the opportunity to take the affair further because he enjoyed it, but on the other hand he wasn't yet clear what fresh twist he should give it. And Törless was effectively paralysed by the mere idea of having to deal with Basini on a daily basis.

When he had uttered the word 'thief', things had for a moment become easier for him. It had been like an expulsion, a driving off of the things that were burrowing away within him.

But the questions that immediately reappeared could not be solved by that simple word. Now that it was no longer possible to avoid them they had become clearer.

Törless looked from Reiting to Beineberg, closed his eyes, repeated to himself the decision he had made, looked up once more ... He himself no longer knew – was it merely his imagination settling on things like an enormous distorting glass, or was it true, did everything really resemble the weird vision he saw before him? And was it only Beineberg and Reiting who knew nothing about these issues? Despite the fact that they were the ones who had, from the start, been at home in this world, which only now, all of a sudden, seemed so strange to him?

Törless was afraid of them. But he was only afraid the way one is afraid of a giant one knows to be blind and stupid ...

But one thing was resolved: He had come a long way from a quarter of an hour before. There was no turning back. He felt a faint curiosity about how things would turn out now that he was held prisoner against his will. Everything that stirred within him remained in darkness, but he already felt a desire to stare into the pattern of that darkness, to which the others were oblivious. A faint shiver mingled with that desire. As though a grey, overcast sky hung constantly over his life – with large clouds, monstrous, changing figures, and the question, repeated time and again: Are they monsters? Are they only clouds?

And that question was for him alone! A secret, something alien to the others, something forbidden ...

So it was that Basini began, for the first time, to approach the significance that he would later assume in Törless's life.

The next day surveillance on Basini began.

Not entirely without ceremony. That morning they skipped gymnastics, held on a large lawn in the grounds.

Reiting delivered a kind of address, and not exactly a brief one. He explained to Basini that he had forfeited his existence, that he should really be reported, and it was only because of a special leniency that he was temporarily escaping the punishment of expulsion.

Then he was informed of the special conditions. Reiting would ensure that they were adhered to.

During the entire performance Basini had been very pale, but he had not uttered a word in reply, and it was impossible to tell from his face what was happening within him.

Törless had found the scene alternately very tasteless and very meaningful.

Beineberg had paid more attention to Reiting than to Basini.

Over the next few days the matter seemed almost to have been forgotten. Except during lessons and at mealtimes Reiting was hardly in evidence, Beineberg was more silent than ever, and Törless continually put off thinking about the matter.

Basini moved around among the schoolmates as though nothing had happened.

He was a little taller than Törless but very puny in build, his movements were mild and languid, his features feminine. He was not intelligent, he was one of the worst at fencing and gymnastics, but he did have a pleasant kind of coquettish charm.

He had only visited Božena on that occasion to act the man. Given his retarded development, any real desire would still have been entirely alien to him. Rather he felt it merely a compulsion, something appropriate or obligatory, to have about him the aura of amatory adventures. He had been happiest when he was leaving Božena and it was all behind him, because all that concerned him was possession of the memory.

Sometimes he lied out of vanity. For example, he came back from holiday with souvenirs of his little affairs – hair-bands, curls, billets-doux. But once when he had brought back a garter in his suitcase, sweet, small, fragrant, sky-blue, and over time it had transpired that it belonged to his twelve-year-old sister, he had been roundly mocked for his ludicrous boasting.

His evident moral inferiority was of a kind with his stupidity. He could not resist any notion that occurred to him, and was always surprised by the consequences. In that he was like those women with pretty little curls over their foreheads, who give their husbands gradual doses of poison in their meals, and are then horrified by the strange, harsh words of the public prosecutor and the death sentence that they receive.

Törless stayed out of his way. As a result he gradually lost the profound inner anxiety which had, from the first, clutched at the roots of his thoughts and shaken him to the core. Törless's life grew rational again; his disconcerted astonishment faded and became more unreal by the day, like the residues of a dream that cannot survive the realities of the solid, sunlit world.

To reassure himself further of this condition, he conveyed all of this in a letter to his parents. But he said nothing of what he himself had felt.

He had now come back round to the view that it was best to ensure that Basini be expelled from the school at the next opportunity. He could not imagine that his parents could think otherwise. What he expected from them was a severe and disgusted condemnation of Basini, as though they were flicking him away with their fingertips like an unclean insect that one could not bear to see near one's son.

There was none of this in the letter that he received in reply.

His parents had taken a great deal of trouble and, as rational people, weighed up all the circumstances, in so far as they were able to form an idea of them from the disjointed and fragmentary communications in that hastily written letter. In the end they advised the greatest caution and reticence, all the more so since their son's depiction of events might well have contained a certain degree of exaggeration produced by youthful indignation. So they approved the decision to give Basini the opportunity to mend his ways, and considered that one should not drive the destiny of a human being off course for the sake of a minor error. All the more so – and they particularly stressed this as being quite obvious – since in this case the people concerned were not complete, but malleable characters grasped in the middle of their development. Certainly, Basini must be treated with all the gravity and strictness that one could muster, but he should always be approached with benevolence and attempts should be made to improve him.

They backed this up this with a series of examples with which Törless was very familiar. Because he very clearly remembered that in the lower forms, on which the authorities still liked to impose draconian moral codes, keeping pocket money within severely restricted limits, some of the little boys, greedy as they all were, could often not keep from begging the more fortunate among them for a bite of their ham sandwich, or whatever it might have been. He himself had occasionally succumbed to this, although he concealed his shame by cursing the wicked and malevolent authorities. And he thanked not only the years, but also the solemn and well-intentioned admonitions of his parents for the fact that he had gradually learned to maintain his pride and avoid such weaknesses.

But none of that had any effect today.

He had to acknowledge that his parents were correct in many respects, and he also knew that it was barely possible to judge accurately from a distance; but something of far greater importance seemed to be missing from their letter.

That was the understanding of the fact that something irrevocable had taken place, something that should never happen among people of a certain class of society. The letter lacked astonishment and shock. They spoke as though this was something normal that had to be resolved with tact, but without becoming over-excited. A stain as unlovely but as unavoidable as one's daily call of nature. There was no more trace of a more personal, unsettled vision than there was in Beineberg and Reiting.

Törless could have taken all this on board. Instead he tore the letter into little pieces and burned it. It was the first time in his life that he was guilty of such a lack of piety.

What had been unleashed within him was the opposite effect to that intended. In contrast to the simple version that they presented to him, all of a sudden he found himself thinking about the problematic, ambiguous aspect of Basini's offence. He said to himself with a shake of the head that further thought on the subject was required, although he could give no precise reason why that should be so ...

The strangest thing occurred when he pursued the matter more in daydreams than in reflection. It was then that Basini struck him as comprehensible and ordinary, clearly outlined, the way his parents and friends saw him: and a moment later he vanished and returned again and again as a tiny figure that sometimes gleamed against a deep, very deep background ...

Then one night – it was very late and everyone was asleep – Törless was shaken awake.

Beineberg was sitting on the edge of his bed. This was so unusual that Törless immediately sensed that something extraordinary must be happening.

'Get up. But don't make a sound, in case anybody notices; we're about to go upstairs, I've got something to tell you.'

Törless quickly dressed, threw on his coat and slipped into his slippers ...

Upstairs, Beineberg took particular care in reassembling all the obstacles, and then prepared some tea.

Törless, his limbs still filled with sleep, contentedly allowed the golden, scented warmth to flow through him. He leaned back in a corner and huddled up; he was waiting for a surprise.

Finally Beineberg said, 'Reiting's going behind our backs.'

Törless wasn't at all surprised; he accepted, as though it was something quite natural, that matters would continue along these lines; he felt almost as though he had merely been waiting for this to happen. Quite involuntarily he said, 'I thought so!'

'Really? You thought so? But surely you can't have noticed anything? That wouldn't be at all like you.'

'Certainly, nothing's struck me; and I haven't given it another thought.'

'I've been paying attention, though; I haven't trusted Reiting from the first moment. You know that Basini gave me my money back. And where do you think he got it? Do you think it was his own? No . . .'

'And you think Reiting might have had a hand in it?'

'I'm sure of it.'

At first Törless could only imagine that Reiting must have got himself involved in something similar.

'So you think that Reiting's been doing what Basini –?'

'The very idea! He took what was necessary from his own money, so that Basini could pay off his debt to me.'

'I can't see any good reason for that.'

'I couldn't either, for a long time. But you too must have noticed the way Reiting was so firmly on Basini's side from the very start. You were absolutely right; it would really have been the most natural thing in the world for the fellow to be expelled. But I deliberately didn't side with you then because I thought to myself: I've got to see what else is going on. I don't really know whether he had any clear intentions then, or whether he just wanted to wait until he was sure of Basini once and for all. Anyway, now I know what's happening.'

'And?'

'Hang on, it'll take a moment to tell you. You know that business in the school four years ago?'

'What business?'

'You know, *that* business!'

'Only vaguely. I just know that there was a big scandal about some beastliness or other, and that a lot of people were thrown out on account of it.'

'That's the one. When I was on holiday I found out more about it from someone who was there. There was a pretty boy in the class and lots of the other boys were in love with him. You'll know about that, it happens in every year. But on this occasion they took it too far.'

'How come?'

'Well . . . because . . . ? Don't ask such stupid questions! And that's what Reiting's doing with Basini!'

Törless immediately understood what was going on, and he felt himself choking as though his throat was full of sand.

'I wouldn't have thought that of Reiting.' It was the best thing he could come up with. Beineberg shrugged his shoulders.

'He thinks he can go behind our backs.'

'Is he in love?'

'Not a trace of it. He's not that much of a fool. It entertains him, or at least it gives him sensual stimulation.'

'And Basini?'

'Basini? . . . Haven't you noticed how cheeky he's been getting lately? He's hardly let me say a word to him. It's always been Reiting this, Reiting that – as if he was his personal guardian angel. He's probably thought it's better to put up with everything from one person than a little from everybody. And Reiting has probably promised to protect him if he agrees to everything. But I think they've made a mistake, and I'm going to get Basini to spill the beans!'

'How did you find all this out?'

'I followed them once.'

'Where?'

'Just next door, in the attic. I'd given Reiting the key to the other entrance. Then I came here, carefully opened the hole and crept across to them.'

A gap had been made in the thin partition wall separating the storeroom from the attic, just wide enough for a human body to push through. It was supposed to serve as an emergency exit in the event of a surprise, and it was usually blocked shut with bricks.

There was a long pause, in which all that could be seen was the glow of tobacco.

Törless couldn't think; he saw . . . All of a sudden he saw a mad swirl of events behind his closed eyes . . . People; people harshly lit, lights and deep-etched, agitated shadows; faces . . . a face; a smile . . . an opening eye . . . a quivering of the skin; he saw people as he had never seen them before, never felt about them before: but he saw them without seeing, without thoughts, without images; as though his soul alone could see them; they were so distinct that he was pierced through by their intensity, but, as though coming to a halt at a threshold that they could not cross, they retreated as soon as he sought words to get them under control.

He couldn't keep from asking more questions. His voice trembled. 'And . . . did you see?'

'Yes?'

'And . . . how was Basini?'

But Beineberg said nothing, and again all that could be heard was the unquiet crackling of the cigarettes. Only after a long time did Beineberg begin to speak again.

'I have given the matter a great deal of thought, and you know I have very particular ideas about the subject. First of all, I don't think Basini matters one bit. Whether we report him now, or beat him, or torture him half to death just for the pleasure of it. Because I can't imagine such a person having any significance in the wonderful mechanism of the world. He seems to me just to have been created at random, apart from the usual way of things. That is – even he must mean something, but only something vague, like a worm or a stone in our path, which we don't know whether to step on or kick aside. And that's as good as nothing. Because if the world-soul wishes one of its parts to be preserved, it says so more clearly. It says no, and creates an obstacle, it makes us walk around the worm, it makes the stone so hard that we can't break it without a hammer. Because by the time we go and get one it will have interposed a host of small, stubborn considerations, and if we can overcome them, then the whole business meant something else from the start.

'Where a human being is concerned, that hardness is in his character, in his consciousness as a person, in his sense of responsibility, being a part of the world-soul. If a person loses that sense, he loses himself. But if a person has lost himself and abandoned himself, he has lost the particular, the actual thing for which nature created him as a person. And one could never be more certain than one is in this case that one is dealing with something unnecessary, with an empty form, with something that was abandoned by the world-soul long ago.'

Törless felt no inclination to contradict. He wasn't paying any great attention. He had never had use for such metaphysical notions, and had never wondered how someone of Beineberg's intelligence could become addicted to this kind of nonsense. The whole issue had never yet fallen within his life's horizon.

Accordingly, he didn't take any trouble to examine the meaning of Beineberg's remarks; he was only half listening.

He just didn't understand how anyone could find such a drawn-out way of approaching a subject like that. Everything in him trembled, and the detailed formality with which Beineberg brought back his ideas from God knows where struck him as ridiculous and inappropriate, it tried his patience. But Beineberg continued in a composed manner: 'The business with Reiting, however, is quite different. By doing what he is doing, he too has played straight into my hands, but I am certainly not as indifferent to his fate as I am to Basini's. His mother has no great fortune, you know; so if he's thrown out of the school, all his plans are at an end. If he starts from here he can make something of himself, but otherwise he would have little chance. And Reiting has never liked me ... do you understand? ... he has always hated me ... he used to try to do me harm whenever he could ... I think he'd even be happy if he could get rid of me today. Now do you see all the things I can do by possessing this secret? ...'

Törless was frightened, and strangely so, as though Reiting's fate also applied to him. He looked in terror at Beineberg. Beineberg had narrowed his eyes to a slit, and looked like a big, sinister spider, lying quietly in wait in its web. To Törless's ears his final words sounded cold and clear, like a decree.

He had not followed what had gone before, and had known only this: Beineberg is talking about his own ideas again, and they have nothing to do with the issue at hand ... and now, all of a sudden, he didn't know how it had happened.

The web that had begun somewhere out in a world of abstraction, as he recalled, must suddenly have contracted with fabulous speed. For all of a sudden it was now concrete, real, alive, and there was a head wriggling in it ... its throat snared shut.

He didn't like Reiting at all, but he now remembered the charming, impudent, free-and-easy manner with which he set up his intrigues, while Beineberg, on the other hand, struck him as shameful, quiet and grinning as he contracted his many-threaded, loathsome grey cocoon of ideas around the other boy.

Törless involuntarily lashed out at him: 'You can't use it against him.' His constant, secret distaste for Beineberg might also have played a part in it.

But after a moment's reflection Beineberg said, of his own accord, 'Why should I? It really would be a pity where he was concerned. In any case, he's not a threat to me any more, and he's too valuable to be allowed to come unstuck over something so stupid.' That was that side of things dealt with. But Beineberg went on talking, and returned to Basini's fate.

'Do you still think we should report Basini?' But Törless didn't reply. He wanted to hear Beineberg speaking, his words sounded to him like the echo of footsteps on hollow earth, and he wanted to enjoy that situation to the full.

Beineberg pursued his thoughts further. 'I think we'll keep him to ourselves for the time being and carry out our own punishment. Because he must be punished – for his arrogance if nothing else. The school authorities would expel him at most, and write a long letter to his uncle – you know how businesslike they are about such things. Your Excellency, your nephew has let himself down . . . bad company . . . return him to your care . . . hope that you will succeed . . . path of improvement . . . impossible for the time being to be with other boys . . . etc. Does a case like that hold any interest or value for them?'

'And what sort of value would it have for us?'

'What sort of value? None for you, perhaps, because you're going to be a government official, or perhaps a poet – you don't need it, maybe you're even scared of it. But I have different plans for my life!'

This time Törless started listening.

'Basini has value for me – very great value, in fact. Because, look – you would just let him off the hook, and you'd be quite satisfied with knowing that he was a bad person.' Törless suppressed a smile. 'That's enough for you, because you have no gift or interest in learning anything from a case such as this. But I am interested. If you have a journey ahead of you, inevitably you see people in quite a different way. So I want to keep Basini, so that I can learn from him.'

'But how do you intend to punish him?'

Beineberg held back his answer for a moment, as though he was still considering the effect he expected from it. Then he said, carefully and hesitantly: 'You're wrong if you think I'm all that concerned with punishing him. We'll have to think of a punishment for him in the end, of course . . . but, to be reasonably brief, I have something else in mind, I want to . . . how shall we put it . . . torment him . . .'

Törless didn't say a word. He still couldn't see everything quite clearly, but he felt that all of this was happening for him as – inwardly – it must. Beineberg, who couldn't see the effect his words were having, continued: '. . . There's no need to be worried, it isn't as bad as all that. Because, as I've just explained to you, there's no need to show any consideration for Basini. Our decision about whether we should spare him or condemn him depends solely on our need for the one or the other. It depends on inner reasons. Do you have any of those? That stuff you came out with about morals, society and all that won't count for anything, of course; I hope you never believed in it yourself. So presumably you don't care either way. But at the same time you can still withdraw from the whole business if you don't want to stake anything on it.

'My own journey won't take me backwards, it won't take me sideways, but straight ahead, and right through the middle. That's the way it must be. Reiting won't drop the matter either, because it's particularly important for him to have a person entirely in his hands and to be able to practise on him, to treat him like a tool. He wants to rule, and would do to you what he's doing to Basini if the opportunity arose. But there's more at stake for me. Almost an obligation to myself; how can I make that difference between us clear to you? You know how Reiting reveres Napoleon: now compare that with the fact that the person who would hold most appeal for me would be more like some sort of philosopher and Indian holy man. Reiting would sacrifice Basini and feel nothing but interest in the process. He would dissect him morally to discover what such an undertaking would involve. And, as I have said, he would deal with you or me just as roundly as he would with Basini, and it wouldn't make the slightest difference to him. On the other hand, just like you, I have this particular feeling that Basini is, in the end, a human being as well. Something in me, too, is injured by any act of cruelty. But that's exactly what this is all about! A sacrifice! You see, I'm fastened to two threads as well. The ill-defined thread that binds me to inaction born of pity, in contrast to my own clear conviction, but also a second one which runs to my soul, to innermost knowledge, and binds me to the cosmos. People like Basini, as I said to you before, mean nothing – they're an empty, accidental form. The only true human beings are those who can penetrate within themselves, cosmic human beings, capable of losing themselves until they connect with the great universal process. They work miracles with their eyes closed, because they are able to use the whole power of the universe, which is within them just as much as it is outside them. But in the past anyone who has pursued the second thread to that point has first had to break the first one. I have read of terrible penances performed by enlightened monks, and you must know something of the methods of the Indian holy men. The sole purpose of all the cruel things that happen is to kill off miserable, outward-directed desires which, whether they be pride or hunger, joy or pity, only pull us away from the fire that each one of us has the potential to start within him.

'Reiting only knows the external, I follow the second thread. Now he has the advantage in most people's eyes, because my journey is slower and more uncertain. But all of a sudden I can overtake him as if he was a worm. You see, it is asserted that the world consists of unshakeable mechanical laws. That is quite false, it's just what it says in schoolbooks! The outside world is stubborn, and up to a certain point its so-called laws cannot be influenced, but some people have succeeded in doing just that. That is written in the holy books that have stood the test of time, and of which most people know nothing at all. From those books I know that there have been people who have been able to move stones and air and water simply by activating their will, and whose prayers were a match for any earthly power. But they too are only the outward triumphs of the spirit. For whoever manages to behold his soul entirely, his physical life, which is merely accidental, dissolves; it says in the books that those people have directly entered a higher realm of the soul.'

Beineberg was speaking entirely seriously, with restrained

excitement. Törless still kept his eyes almost uninterruptedly closed; he felt Beineberg's breath reaching across to him, and absorbed it like an oppressive anaesthetic. Meanwhile Beineberg was concluding his speech:

'So you can see what it is that concerns me. That which persuades me to let Basini go is of base, external origin. You may pursue it. For me it is a prejudice of which I must rid myself, as I must of everything that distracts me from the journey into my innermost depths.

'The very fact that it is difficult for me to torment Basini – I mean, to humiliate him, to oppress him, to drive him from me – is a good thing. It requires a sacrifice. It will be purifying. I owe it to myself to learn daily from him that merely to be human means nothing at all – a merely aping, outward likeness.'

Törless didn't understand everything. He just had the idea, once again, that an invisible noose had suddenly contracted into a tangible, fatal knot. Beineberg's last words echoed within him. 'A merely aping, outward likeness,' he repeated to himself. The same thing also seemed to apply to his relationship with Basini. Did the strange attraction that Basini exerted upon him not lie in visions of that kind? Simply in the fact that he could not enter Basini's thoughts, and therefore always sensed him as though in vague images? When he had previously imagined Basini, had there not been a second, blurred face behind the first, one that bore a tangible likeness, although one could not have said to what?

Thus it happened that Törless, rather than reflecting upon Beineberg's very curious intentions, half dazed by his new and unfamiliar impressions, tried to have a clear understanding of himself. He remembered the afternoon before he had learned of Basini's offence. Those visions had actually been there then. There had always been something that his thoughts could not deal with. Something that seemed so simple and so strange. He had seen images that were not images. Outside those hovels, even when he was sitting with Beineberg in the cake shop.

There were similarities and unbridgeable dissimilarities. And he had been excited by this game, this secret, very personal perspective.

And now one human being was monopolizing it all. Everything had now become real, embodied in a single human being. And so all the strangeness was transferred to that one human being. In the process it sprang out of the imagination and into life, and grew threatening . . .

All the excitement had exhausted Törless, his thoughts were only loosely linked together.

All that remained with him was the memory that he could not let Basini go, that Basini was destined to play an important role for him too, and one which he had as yet only vaguely discerned.

In the meantime he shook his head in amazement as he thought of Beineberg's words. Was he, too . . . ?

He can't be searching for the same thing as me, and yet he was the one who found the right term for it . . .

Törless was dreaming rather than thinking. He was no longer capable of distinguishing his own psychological problem from Beineberg's fantasies. In the end he had only a single feeling, that the giant noose was contracting ever tighter around everything.

The conversation went no further. They put out the light and crept carefully back into their dormitory.

The next few days brought no decision. There was a lot of school work to be done, Reiting carefully avoided being on his own, and Beineberg too was cautious not to return to their discussion.

Thus it came about that during these days, like a stream driven underground, what had happened buried its way deeper into Törless and gave his thoughts an irrevocable direction.

There was no longer any question of having Basini expelled. Now, for the first time, Törless felt wholly concentrated upon himself, and was unable to think of anything else. He even felt indifferent about Božena; what he had felt for her was becoming a fantastic memory, which had now made way for something serious.

Admittedly that serious thing seemed to be no less fantastic.

Preoccupied with his thoughts, Törless had gone for a walk alone in the school grounds. It was about midday, and the late autumn sun cast pale memories over meadows and paths. Since Törless, unsettled as he was, did not feel like walking any further, he merely strolled around the building and threw himself down in the pale, rustling grass at the foot of the almost windowless side wall. The sky spread out above him, in that pale, ailing blue so typical of autumn, and little white round clouds scudded across it.

Törless lay stretched out on his back and, dreaming vaguely, squinted between two treetops in front of him that were shedding their leaves.

He thought of Beineberg; what a strange character he was! His words would have been at home in a crumbling Indian temple, among weird idols and serpents lurking in deep crannies, initiated into the secrets of magic; but what place did they have in the daylight, in the institute, in modern Europe? And yet those words, having snaked their way endlessly in a thousand twists and turns, like a path without end or view, seemed suddenly to have reached a tangible goal . . .

And suddenly he noticed – and he felt as though this was happening for the first time – how high the sky really was.

It came to him like a shock. Right above him there gleamed a little blue, unimaginably deep hole between the clouds.

It seemed to him that if one had a long, long ladder, one should be able to climb into that hole. But the further he pushed his way in, lifting himself up with his gaze, the further away the blue, glowing background retreated. And yet he felt as though it should be possible to reach it and hold it, merely with one's gaze. The desire became painfully intense.

It was as though the power of vision, strained to its limit, was flinging glances like arrows between the clouds, and as though, aim as far as they might, they always fell short.

Törless thought about this now; he tried to remain as calm and sensible as he possibly could. 'Of course there is no end,' he said to himself, 'it goes on and on, ever onward, into infinity.' He kept his eyes fixed on the sky and said this out loud, as though to test the power of a magic spell. But without success; the words said nothing, or rather they said something quite different, as though they were referring to the same object, but to another strange, indifferent side of it.

'Infinity!' Törless knew the word from maths class. He had never imagined anything particular by it. It was forever returning; someone must have invented it once, and since then it had become possible to calculate with it as surely as one did with anything solid. It was whatever its value happened to be in the calculation; Törless had never ventured further than that.

And now, all of a sudden, the idea flashed through him that there was something terribly unsettling about the word. It struck him as a concept that had formerly been tamed, one with which he had performed his daily little tricks, and which had now been suddenly unleashed. Something beyond understanding, something wild and destructive seemed to have been put to sleep by the work of some clever inventor, and had now suddenly been woken to life, and grown terrible before him. There, in that sky, it now stood vividly above him and menaced and mocked.

Finally he closed his eyes, because the vision tormented him so.

Soon after that, awoken by a gust of wind that rustled through the dry grass, he could barely feel his body, and a pleasant coolness flowed up from his feet, keeping his limbs in a state of sweet languor. Something mild and tired now mingled with his former fear. He still felt the sky staring down on him, vast and silent, but now he recalled how often he had had such an impression in the past, and as though in a state between waking and dreaming he ran through all of those memories, and felt as though all their associations were spinning him into a cocoon.

First of all there was that childhood memory in which the trees had stood as serious and silent as enchanted people. Even then he must have had that feeling that later returned to him again and again. Something of it had even been present in the thoughts he had had at Božena's, a particular foreboding, something more than those thoughts suggested. And that moment of silence in the garden outside the windows of the cake shop, before the dark veils of sensuality had fallen, that had been like that too. And Beineberg and Reiting had often, within the fragment of a thought, become something alien and unreal; and finally, what about Basini? The idea of what was about to happen to him had utterly torn Törless in two; one moment it was reasonable and ordinary, the next it had assumed that same silence, with images flashing through it, which had gradually seeped into Törless's perception and now, all of a sudden, demanded to be treated as something real and alive; just as the idea of infinity had done before.

Törless now felt that silence surrounding him on all sides. Like distant, dark forces, it had probably been threatening for ever, but he had instinctively retreated from it, and had only shyly glanced at it from time to time. But now an accident, an event, had sharpened his attention and focused it upon it, and as if responding to a sign it was now crashing in from all sides, bringing with it a terrible confusion that spread further with each new moment.

It came upon Törless like a madness, experiencing objects, processes and people as things with ambiguous meanings. As something fettered by some inventor's power to a harmless, explanatory word, and as something wholly alien that seemed at every moment to threaten to break its bonds.

Certainly: there is a simple, natural explanation for everything, and Törless knew that too, but to his fearful astonishment it only seemed to rip away an outermost shell without laying bare the interior, which Törless, as though with eyes by now unnatural, saw always glimmering as a second layer behind it.

Törless lay there, entirely wrapped in a cocoon of memories, from which alien thoughts grew like strange blossoms. Those moments that no one forgets, situations in which there is a failure of the associations that normally allow us to reflect our lives whole within our understanding, as though the two things were running along side by side and at the same speed – coming confusingly close to one another.

The memory of the terribly still, sad-coloured silence of certain evenings alternated suddenly with the hot, tremulous unease of a summer afternoon that had once rippled glowing across his soul, as though with the twitching feet of a hissing swarm of glittering lizards.

Then he suddenly remembered a smile of that young prince – a glance – a movement – from the time when they had profoundly broken with one another – with which the prince had suddenly – gently – freed himself from all the connections that Törless had spun around him – and stepped into a new and strange expanse which – as though concentrated into the life of a single indescribable second – had opened up unexpectedly. Then once more there came memories from the wood – between the fields. Then a silent picture in a gloomy room at home, which had later suddenly reminded him of his lost friend. Words from a poem came to mind . . .

And there are other things too, governed by that incommensurability of experience and understanding. But it is always the case that what we experience in one moment, whole and unquestioning, becomes incomprehensible and confused when we seek to bind it to our enduring ownership with the chains of thought. And what looks big and inhuman while our words reach it from afar, becomes simple and ceases to be unsettling the moment it enters our life's field of action.

*

And so all those memories suddenly shared a single secret. As though they all belonged together, they stood clearly before him, within his grasp.

When they had happened, they had been accompanied by an obscure emotion to which he had paid little attention.

That was precisely what he was trying to do now. It struck him that he had once, standing with his father before one of those landscapes, cried out unexpectedly: 'Oh, how beautiful that is' – and had been embarrassed by his father's pleasure. On that occasion he might just as easily have said: 'How terribly sad it is.' It was a failure of words that tormented him then, a half-awareness that the words were merely random excuses for what he had felt.

And today he remembered the picture, he remembered the words, and he clearly recalled lying about that feeling even though he did not know why. His eye ran through everything again in his memory. But it returned unassuaged, again and again. A smile of delight at the wealth of ideas that he still clutched as though distractedly, slowly assumed a barely perceptible, painful trait . . .

He felt the need to persist in his search for a bridge, a context, a comparison – between himself and that which stood silently before his mind.

But however often he had calmed himself with a thought, that incomprehensible objection remained: you're lying. It was as though he had to pass through an unstoppable division of soldiers, a stubborn remnant forever leaping out at him, or as though he was wearing his feverish fingers raw trying to undo an endless knot.

And finally he gave up. The room closed in around him, and his memories burgeoned in unnatural distortions.

He had set his eyes on the sky once more. As though by chance he might be able to wrench its secret from it, and guess from it what it was that everywhere confused him. But he grew tired, and the feeling of deep loneliness closed over him. The sky was silent. And Törless felt he was completely alone beneath that mute, motionless arch; he felt like a little living dot beneath that vast, transparent corpse.

But it barely frightened him any more. By now it had seized hold of his last limb, like an old, familiar pain.

He felt as though the light had assumed a milky glow, and was dancing before his eyes like a pale, cold mist.

Slowly and carefully he turned his head and looked around to see if everything had really changed. Then his gaze brushed past the grey, windowless wall behind his head. It seemed to have leaned over him, and to be looking at him in silence. From time to time a trickling sound descended, and a weird life awoke in the wall.

He had often listened to it like that in the hiding place, as Beineberg and Retting unfurled their fantastic world, and he had enjoyed it as one might enjoy the strange background music to some grotesque drama.

But now the bright daylight itself seemed to have become an inexplicable hiding place, and vivid silence surrounded Törless on all sides.

He couldn't turn his head away. Beside him, in a damp, dark corner, coltsfoot flourished, its broad leaves spreading into fantastic hiding places for snails and worms.

Törless heard the beating of his heart. Then, again, there came a quiet trickling, a whispering, a seeping away . . . And those sounds were the only living things in a timeless and silent world . . .

The next day Beineberg was standing with Reiting when Törless walked over to them.

'I've had a word with Reiting,' said Beineberg, 'and sorted everything out. You won't really be interested in anything like this.'

Törless felt something like anger and jealousy welling up in him about this sudden turn of events, but he didn't know whether he should mention the night-time conversation in front of Reiting. 'Well, you could at least have called me about it, since I'm just as involved as you are,' he said.

'And we would have done, my dear Törless,' Reiting hastened to say, now clearly concerned to avoid any unnecessary difficulties, 'but we couldn't find you and we assumed you would agree. What's your own opinion of Basini, by the way?' (Not a word of apology, as though his own behaviour was self-explanatory.)

'Basini? Well, he's just a rotten swine,' Törless said, embarrassed.

'He is, isn't he? Rotten indeed.'

'But you're getting yourself into a bit of a mess!' And Törless forced a smile, ashamed not to be angrier with Reiting.

'Me?' Reiting shrugged his shoulders. 'So what? You should try everything in life, and if he's so stupid and so pitiful –'

'Have you had another word with him?' Beineberg interrupted.

'Yes; he was in my room last night asking for money, because he has debts he can't pay again.'

'Did you let him have it?'

'No, not yet.'

'That's terrific,' said Beineberg, 'it means we have the opportunity we've been waiting for to grab him. You could arrange to meet him somewhere tonight.'

'Where? The storeroom?'

'I don't think so, I'd rather he didn't know anything about it for the time being. But tell him to come up to the attic, where you were with him before.'

'For what time?'

'Let's say . . . eleven.'

'Fine. – Do you want to go for a walk?'

'Yes. I expect Törless still has some homework to do, doesn't he?'

Törless had no more work to do, but he felt that the two of them were sharing something that they wanted to hide from him. He was annoyed at his formality, which kept him from getting involved.

So he looked jealously after them and imagined all the things that they might have secretly arranged between them.

And it struck him that there was an innocuous charm in Reiting's upright, fluent walk – just as there was in his words. And against that he tried to imagine him as he must have been that evening; inwardly, mentally. It must have been like a long, slow sinking of two particular souls, and then the depth of a subterranean kingdom – and in between a moment in which the sounds of the world, above, far above, fell silent and were extinguished.

Can a person ever be so content and light again after something of that kind? Clearly it didn't mean that much to him. Törless would so much have liked to ask him. And instead he had, with childlike timidity, handed him over to that spidery character Beineberg!

At a quarter to eleven Törless saw Beineberg and Reiting slipping from their beds and getting dressed straight away.

'Psst! – just wait a minute. People will notice if we all go off at the same time.'

Törless hid back under his covers.

Then they met up in the corridor and climbed towards the attic with their usual caution.

'Where's Basini?' asked Törless.

'He's coming up from the other direction; Reiting gave him the key.'

All the way up they stayed in darkness. Only once they were upstairs, by the big iron door, did Beineberg light his little signalling lantern.

The lock was resistant. It had been unused for years, and refused to obey the copied key. Finally it fell back with a hard sound; the heavy door rubbed reluctantly in the rust of the hinges, and hesitantly yielded.

A warm, stale air rushed from the attic, like the air that comes from small greenhouses.

Beineberg closed the door again.

They descended the little wooden steps and crouched down next to a massive crossbeam.

Beside them were huge bottles of water that were supposed to act as extinguishers if a fire broke out. The water in them had clearly not been replaced for ages, and gave off a sweetish smell.

The whole environment was extremely oppressive: the heat under the roof, the bad air and the creaking of the massive beams, some of them disappearing upwards to lose themselves in the dark, some of them creeping down to the floor in a ghostly criss-cross.

Beineberg turned the lamp down, and they sat, not saying a word, motionless in the darkness – for many minutes.

Then, at the other end, the door creaked in the dark. Quiet and hesitant. It was a sound that made the heart leap into the throat, like the first sound of approaching prey.

Other, uncertain steps followed, the sound of a foot against groaning wood; a dull sound, as though of a body striking something . . . Silence . . . Then, again, tentative steps . . . Waiting . . . A quiet, human sound . . . 'Reiting?'

Then Beineberg took the cap off the signalling lamp and cast a wide beam of light towards the place where the voice was coming from.

A few massive beams lit up with sharp shadows, and for a while nothing could be seen but a cone of dancing dust.

But the steps grew more definite and came closer.

Then – very close – another foot fell against the wood, and in the next moment, in the broad base of the cone of light, they saw – ash-pale in the murky light – Basini's face.

Basini was smiling. A friendly, sweet smile. Rigidly fixed, like the smile in a painting, it rose out of the light's frame.

Törless sat pressed against his beam, and felt the muscles in his eyes twitching.

Now Beineberg listed Basini's disgraceful deeds; evenly, his voice hoarse.

Then came the question: 'So, aren't you at all ashamed?' Then a glance from Basini to Reiting, apparently saying, 'Now it's time for you to help me.' And at that moment Reiting struck Basini in the face with his fist, so that he tottered backwards, stumbled against a beam and fell. Beineberg and Reiting jumped after him.

The lamp had tipped over, and its light flowed, uncomprehending and lethargic, across the floor to Törless's feet . . .

From the sounds that reached him, Törless could make out that they were taking Basini's clothes from his body and whipping him with something thin and flexible. They had clearly had all this prepared. He heard Basini's whimpering and muted complaints, incessantly begging for mercy; finally all he heard was a groan, like suppressed weeping, and occasional muffled curses and Beineberg's hot, passionate breathing.

He had not moved from his spot. At first he had been seized by a bestial desire to leap in with the others and deliver the beating, but he was restrained by the feeling that he was too late, that he would be superfluous. Paralysis lay heavy over his limbs.

He looked at the floor in front of him with apparent indifference. He didn't pitch his hearing to follow the sounds, and he didn't feel his heart beating more quickly than usual. With his eyes he followed the light that poured into a lake at his feet. Flecks of dust lit up, and an ugly little spider's web. The beam of light went on seeping into the gaps between the beams and suffocated in a dusty, dirty gloom.

Törless would have spent an hour sitting like that without noticing. He wasn't thinking about anything, and yet internally he was extremely busy. He was observing himself. But only as though he was really looking into the void, as though he was only seeing himself sideways-on, in a vague glow. Now, out of this vagueness – from the side – slowly, but ever more visibly, a desire was clearly emerging into consciousness.

Something made Törless smile. Then the desire grew even stronger. It drew him down from his seat – on to his knees; on to the floor. It drove him to press his body against the boards; he felt his eyes growing large like a fish's eyes, he felt his heart knocking against the wood through his naked body.

Now there really was a massive excitement within Törless, and he had to cling to a beam to brace himself against the vertigo that was drawing him down.

Beads of sweat stood out on his brow, and he asked himself anxiously what all this could possibly mean.

Startled out of his apathy, he started listening out for the others through the darkness.

It had grown quiet over there; only Basini moaning quietly to himself as he felt for his clothes.

Törless felt pleasantly touched by those moaning sounds. A shudder ran up and down his back, as though on the feet of spiders; then it settled between his shoulder-blades and, with delicate claws, drew his scalp backwards. To his disgust Törless realized that he was in a state of sexual arousal. He thought back, and without being able to remember when it had started, he knew that it had accompanied that curious desire to press himself against the floor. It made him ashamed; but it had filled his head like a surging wave of blood.

Beineberg and Reiting felt their way back and sat down silently beside him. Beineberg looked at the lamp.

In that moment Törless was pulled back down again. It emanated from his eyes – he could feel that now – it went from his eyes, like a hypnotic stiffness, to his brain. It was a question, a ... no, a desperation ... oh, how well he knew it ... the wall, the visitors' garden, the low hovels, that childhood memory ... it was the same! the same! He looked at Beineberg. 'Doesn't he feel anything?' he wondered. But Beineberg bent down to pick up the lamp. Törless held his arm back. 'Isn't that like an eye?' he said, pointing to the beam of light flowing over the floor.

'Are you getting poetic now?'

'No. But don't you say yourself that the eyes have a special explanation of their own? They emanate – you just have to think of those hypnotic ideas you love so much – amongst other things they emanate a power that would have no place in a physics lesson – and it's certainly also the case that you can often tell much more about a person from his eyes than from his words . . .'

'And? – So?'

'I see this light as being like an eye. Through to a strange world. I feel as though I'm supposed to guess something from it. But I can't. I'd like to absorb it into me . . .'

'So – you are starting to get poetic.'

'No, I'm serious. I'm quite desperate. Take a close look, and you'll feel it too. A need to splash about in that pool – on all fours, creeping into the dusty corners, as though you could guess it that way . . .'

'My dear boy, that's nonsense, sentimentality. You want to leave that kind of thing alone.'

Beineberg bent all the way down and put the lamp back in its place. But Törless felt a malicious pleasure. He felt that in a sense he was absorbing these events more fully than his companions were.

Now he waited for Basini to reappear, and felt, with a secret shudder, that his scalp was once again being stretched by delicate claws.

He already knew very clearly that something had been saved up for him, something that admonished him again and again, at ever shorter intervals; a sensation that was incomprehensible to the others, but was clearly very important for his life.

He didn't know what his burst of sensuality had to do with it, but he remembered that it had always been present when events had begun to seem strange to him alone, and tormented him because he knew of no reason why that should be.

And he intended to give the matter some serious thought at the next opportunity. For the time being he abandoned himself entirely to the exciting shudder that preceded Basini's reappearance.

Beineberg had set up the lamp, and once again its beams cut a circle into the darkness, like an empty frame.

And all of a sudden Basini's face was in it again; just as it had been the first time; with the same rigidly fixed, sweet smile; as though nothing had happened in the meantime, except that over his upper lip, his mouth and his chin slow drops of blood marked out a red path like a twisting worm.

'Sit down over there!' Reiting pointed to the massive wooden beam. Basini obeyed. Reiting began to speak. 'You probably thought you'd wriggled out of this one, didn't you? You thought I'd help you? Well, you were wrong. I was just trying to see how low you would go.'

Basini made a dismissive gesture. Reiting threatened to jump on him again. Then Basini said, 'I beg you, for God's sake, I had no other choice.'

'Shut up!' shouted Reiting. 'We've had enough of your excuses! We now know once and for all what your situation is, and we're going to act accordingly . . .'

There was a short silence. Then, all of a sudden, Törless said quietly, almost kindly, 'Say: I'm a thief.'

Basini made big, almost terrified eyes; Beineberg laughed comfortably.

But Basini said nothing. Then Beineberg gave him a poke in the ribs and shouted at him:

'Don't you hear? You're to say that you're a thief! Say it right now!'

Once again there was a short, barely noticeable silence. Then Basini said quietly, in a single breath and with the most innocuous emphasis he could muster: 'I'm a thief.'

Beineberg laughed delightedly over at Törless. 'That was a good idea of yours, little one,' and to Basini: 'And right now you're going to say: I'm a beast, a thieving beast, *your* thieving, swinish beast!'

And Basini said it, without hesitation, his eyes closed.

But Törless had already leaned back in the dark again. He was repelled by the scene, and ashamed that he had let the others have his idea.

During maths class Törless had suddenly had an idea.

Over the past few days he had been following his lessons with special interest, thinking, 'If this is really a preparation for life, as they say it is, then it must contain a trace of whatever it is that I'm searching for.'

He had been thinking specifically in terms of mathematics, still pondering the notion of infinity.

And sure enough, in the middle of the lesson, it had burned its way swiftly into his mind. Straight after class he sat down with Beineberg, the only person he could talk to about this kind of thing.

'Did you understand all that?'

'What?'

'All that stuff about imaginary numbers?'

'Yes. It's not all that difficult. You just have to bear in mind that the unit of calculation is the square root of minus one.'

'But that's just it. It doesn't exist. Any number, whether it's positive or negative, gives a positive when it's squared. So there can't be such a thing as a real number that's the square root of something negative.'

'Quite right; but why shouldn't you try to apply the operation of square root calculation to a negative number anyway? It can't produce a real value, of course, and that's why the result is called imaginary. It's as if you were to say: someone always used to sit here, so let's put out a chair for him today; and, even if he's died in the meantime, let's act as though he was going to turn up.'

'But how can you do that if you know for certain, mathematically for certain, that it's impossible?'

'You do it anyway, as if it wasn't the case. You'll have some degree of success. In what way are the so-called irrational numbers different? A division that never comes to an end, a fraction whose value never, ever comes out how ever long you spend on the calculation? And what do you think about parallel lines meeting in infinity? I reckon that if you were too conscientious there would be no maths at all.'

'You're right about that. If you think of it that way it's strange enough. But the curious thing is that, in spite of this, you really can calculate with such imaginary or otherwise impossible values, and you have a tangible result in the end!'

'Well, in order for that to happen, the imaginary factors must cancel one another out in the course of the calculation.'

'Yes, yes; I know what you're saying. But isn't there still something very strange about it all? How should I put it? Just think about it for a moment: in that kind of calculation you have very solid figures at the beginning, which can represent metres or weights or something similarly tangible, and which are at least real numbers. And there are real numbers at the end of the calculation as well. But they're connected to one another by something that doesn't exist. Isn't that like a bridge consisting only of the first and last pillars, and yet you walk over it as securely as though it was all there? For me there's something dizzying about a calculation like that; as if it goes off God knows where for part of the way. But the really uncanny thing about it is the strength that exists in such a calculation, holding you so firmly that you land safely in the end.'

Beineberg grinned: 'You're starting to sound like our chaplain: "... You see an apple – that's light vibrations and the eye and so on – and you reach out your hand to steal it – that's the muscles and the nerves that set it in motion. – But between the two there is something that produces the one from the other – and that is the immortal soul, which has sinned in the process ... yes – yes – none of your actions is explicable without the soul, which plays upon you as it might on the keys of a piano ... !"' And he imitated the intonation with which the cleric liked to deliver that old simile. – 'By the way, the whole business doesn't interest me that much.'

'I thought it would interest you, of all people. At least, I thought of you straight away because – if it really is so inexplicable – it's almost a confirmation of your belief.'

'Why shouldn't it be inexplicable? I think it's entirely possible that the inventors of mathematics were stumbling over their own feet when they were doing this. Because why should whatever lies outside our intellect not be allowed a bit of fun with that same intellect? I'm not going to go into that, though, because these things lead nowhere.'

The same day Törless had asked his maths master if he could visit him to have some passages from his last lecture explained.

The next day, at lunchtime, he climbed the stairs to the master's little apartment.

He now had a quite new respect for mathematics, since it seemed all of a sudden to have turned unexpectedly from a dead chore into something very much alive. And because of that respect he felt a kind of envy for his teacher, who must surely be familiar with all those relationships, and who carried his knowledge of them around with him wherever he went, like the key to a locked garden. Apart from this, though, Törless was also spurred on by a rather hesitant curiosity. He had never been in the room of an adult young man, and he was excited to learn how the life of another, knowledgeable and yet settled person might look, at least as far as one could tell from his outward surroundings.

He was normally shy and reticent with his teachers, and thought that for this reason he did not enjoy their particular affection. So his request seemed to him, as he held his breath with excitement outside the door, to be quite daring, less concerned with receiving enlightenment – because even now he quietly doubted that he would receive it – than with the opportunity to cast a glance behind the teacher, so to speak, and into his daily cohabitation with mathematics.

He was led into the study. It was a long room with a single window; a desk scattered with ink stains stood close to the window, and by the wall there was a sofa covered with a green ribbed fabric, scratchy and tasselled. Above the sofa hung a faded mortarboard and a number of brown, darkened photographs, in visiting-card format, from university days. On the oval table with its x-shaped feet, whose supposedly graceful flourishes looked like an unhappy attempt at elegance, lay a pipe and some coarse, leafy shag. The whole room smelled of cheap tobacco.

Törless had barely absorbed these impressions and become aware of a certain unease in himself, as though he was touching something disagreeable, when his teacher entered the room.

He was a young man of thirty at most, fair-haired and nervous and a very capable mathematician, who had already delivered several important treatises to the Academy.

He immediately sat down at his desk, rummaged around for a moment in the papers scattered around the place (it later occurred to Törless that he had immediately sought refuge in them), cleaned his pince-nez with his handkerchief, laid one leg over the other and looked expectantly at Törless.

Törless had now started to look at him as well. He noticed a pair of rough, white woollen socks and registered that above them the rims of the teacher's long johns had been blackened by boot polish.

On the other hand his handkerchief looked white and elegant, and his tie was stitched together, but made up for this by being splendidly gaudy and chequered like a painter's palette.

Instinctively, Törless felt further repelled by these little observations; he could hardly hope that such a person might really possess any significant knowledge, when quite clearly none of it could be detected in his personal appearance or anywhere in his surroundings. Privately, he had had quite a different idea of what a mathematician's study might be like; that it might somehow express the terrible things that were thought there. The ordinariness of it all wounded him; he transferred that hurt to mathematics in general, and his respect began to make way for a suspicious resistance.

As the teacher rocked back and forth impatiently in his seat, unsure how to interpret the long silence and the watching eyes, there was already a mood of misunderstanding between them.

'Now shall we ... will you ... I'm happy to give you any information you might need,' the teacher began.

Törless set out his reservations and tried to explain their significance for him. But it was as though he was speaking through a thick, dull fog, and the best things he wanted to say stuck in his throat.

The teacher smiled, gave a slight cough, said, 'If you will excuse me,' and lit a cigarette, smoking it in quick puffs; the cigarette paper – and Törless took all this in, finding it very common – was greasy and rustled every time it was rolled; the teacher took his pince-nez from his nose, put it back on again, nodded his head ... in the end he wouldn't let Törless finish.

'I'm glad, my dear Törless, I'm really very glad,' he interrupted. 'Your concerns show that you are serious, they show evidence of independent thought ... of ... hmm ... but it isn't at all easy to give you the explanation you're after ... you mustn't misunderstand me.

'You see, you were talking about the intervention of transcendent, hmm yes ... they're called transcendent – factors ...

'Now I don't know how you feel about this; the supersensory, everything that lies beyond the strict laws of reason, is something that follows its own rules. I'm not really equipped to talk about it, it isn't part of my subject; you can think about it in one way or another, and I would prefer to avoid being controversial ... But where mathematics is concerned, it is quite certain that even here there exists only a natural, purely mathematical context.

'Now – to be strictly scientific – I would have to set out preconditions that you would barely understand, and we haven't time for that anyway.

'You know, I happily concede that for example these numerical values which don't really exist, ha ha, are no small nut for a young student to crack. You will have to accept that such mathematical concepts are purely mathematical logical necessities. Just think for a moment: at the elementary stage of education, which is where you are at present, it is very difficult to find the correct explanation for many of the things that you will encounter. Fortunately very few students are affected by this, but if someone, as you have done today – and, as I say, I am very pleased – does come and ask, one can only say: my dear friend, you must simply believe; if you can do ten times as much mathematics as you do at the moment, you will understand, but for the time being: believe!

'That is the only way, my dear Törless; mathematics is a whole world in itself, and one must have lived in it for a very long time to feel everything that is necessary within it.'

Törless was pleased when the master stopped speaking. Since hearing the door close behind him he had felt that the words were coming from further and further away ... moving towards that other, indifferent side, where all correct yet meaningless explanations lie.

But he was numbed by the torrent of words and by failure, and he didn't immediately understand that he was now expected to rise to his feet.

Then his teacher, in order to resolve matters once and for all, reached for one final persuasive argument.

On a little desk lay an elegant and expensive volume of Kant. The teacher picked it up and showed it to Törless. 'You see this book, this is philosophy, it contains the defining aspects of our actions. And if you could feel your way to the bottom of it, you would encounter only such logical necessities, which define everything despite the fact that they themselves cannot be understood without further ado. It's very much the same with mathematics. And yet we are constantly acting according to those necessities; there you have the proof of how important such things are. But,' he smiled when he saw that Törless was actually opening the book and flicking through it, 'forget that for now. I just wanted to give you an example that you would remember in later years; it would be too difficult for you for the time being.'

All the rest of that day Törless was in an agitated state.

The fact that he had held Kant in his hand – that quite arbitrary fact, to which he had paid little attention at the time – subsequently affected him very powerfully. He knew the name Kant from hearsay, and for him it had the market value that it generally enjoys among those people who only ever come into remote contact with arts subjects – as the last word in philosophy. And that authority had even been one reason why Törless had hitherto paid so little attention to serious books. Once past the phase of wanting to be a coachman, a gardener or a pastry-maker, very young people tend at first, in their mind's eye, to stake out the area of their future life's work wherever their ambition finds the greatest likelihood of achieving excellence. If they say they want to be a doctor, it is sure to mean that at some point they have seen a nicely appointed waiting-room full of people, or a glass case filled with grisly surgical instruments, or something of the kind; if they speak of a diplomatic career, they are thinking of the brilliance and elegance of the international salons: in short, they choose a profession according to the milieu in which they would most like to see themselves, and according to the pose in which they feel they look their best.

Now Törless had only ever heard the name of Kant uttered occasionally and then with a curious expression, as though it was the name of some sinister holy man. And Törless could only imagine that Kant had solved the problems of philosophy once and for all, and that since that time those problems had been merely a pointless occupation, just as he believed that there was no point in writing poetry after Schiller and Goethe.

At home those books were kept in the cupboard with the green glass panes in Papa's study, and Törless knew that the cupboard was never opened except to be shown to a visitor. It was like the sanctum of a deity which one approaches unwillingly, a deity which one worships only because one is happy that, because it exists, there are certain things that one need no longer worry about.

That skewed relationship towards philosophy and literature would later have an unfortunate influence on Törless's further development, and one which would bring him many unhappy hours. It was because it diverted his ambition from its proper objects, and, robbed of his goal, he sought a new one, that he came under the defining and brutal influence of his companions. His tendencies returned only occasionally and shamefacedly, and each time they did so they left behind an awareness that he was doing something ludicrous and pointless. But the inclinations were so strong that he was unable to free himself from them entirely, and this constant struggle robbed his being of its clear outlines and its upright posture.

Today, however, that relationship seemed to have entered a new phase. The ideas about which he had been vainly seeking enlightenment were no longer the rootless associations of a playful imagination. Instead they churned him up, they wouldn't let him go, and he felt with his whole body that an element of his life pulsed away behind them. This was something quite new for Törless. There was a determination within him that he had never known before. It was almost dreamlike, mysterious. It must have been quietly developing under his recent influences, and now all of a sudden it was knocking imperiously. He felt like a mother who feels, for the first time, the peremptory motions of her unborn child.

It was a wonderfully pleasurable afternoon.

From his trunk Törless fetched all the poetic experiments he had stored there. He sat down with them by the stove, and stayed all alone, unseen behind the massive screen. He flicked through one volume after another, then tore each one very slowly into very small pieces and threw them all, one by one, into the fire, each time relishing the tender emotion of farewell.

He was trying to throw all his earlier baggage behind him, as though – unencumbered – he would from now on have to devote all his attention to the steps that would carry him onwards.

Finally he stood up and walked over to join the others. He felt free of all anxious sidelong glances. What he had done had occurred entirely instinctively; nothing offered him any certainty that he might really be someone new from now on, nothing but the mere existence of that impulse. 'Tomorrow,' he said to himself, 'tomorrow I shall carefully revise everything, and I shall acquire clarity.'

He walked around the classroom, between the desks, looked into the open school books, at the fingers hurrying busily back and forth over the dazzling white as they wrote, each carrying its little brown shadow behind it – he watched it all like someone who has suddenly woken up, with eyes to which everything seems of grave significance.

But the very next day brought a terrible disappointment. In the morning Törless had actually bought the cheap edition of the volume he had seen in his teacher's room, and he used his first break-time to start reading it. But filled as it was with parentheses and footnotes, he couldn't understand a word, and when he conscientiously followed the sentences with his eyes, he felt as though an old, bony hand was twisting his brain out of his head.

By the time he stopped, exhausted, after about half an hour, he had only reached the second page, and there was sweat on his brow.

But then he clenched his teeth and read another page until break-time was over.

But in the evening he didn't want to touch the book again. Fear? Nausea? – he wasn't sure. Only one thing was a source of raging torment: that the teacher, that person who didn't look in any way special, had had the book lying open in his room, as though it was a daily source of entertainment.

It was in that mood that Beineberg found him.

'So, Törless, how were things with the maths teacher yesterday?' They were sitting alone in a window-niche, and had pushed in front of it the broad clothes-stands, with all the coats hanging on them, so that all that reached them from the class was a hum that rose and fell and the reflection of the lamps on the ceiling. Törless played distractedly with a coat hanging in front of him.

'Are you asleep? He must have given you an answer of some kind? I can imagine, by the way, that he must have been pretty confused.'

'Why?'

'Well, he won't have been prepared for such a stupid question.'

'It wasn't a stupid question; I still haven't sorted it out.'

'I don't mean that in a nasty way; but it will have been stupid for him. They learn their subjects off by heart the way the vicar learns his catechism, and if you ask them something slightly in the wrong order they always get confused.'

'Oh, he wasn't confused about the answer. He didn't even let me finish, he had it to hand so quickly.'

'And how did he explain the matter?'

'Actually he didn't. He said I wouldn't be able to understand it yet, it was all about logical necessities, which only become clear to someone who has gone into these things more deeply.'

'That's exactly what's fraudulent about it! They can't tell their stories to someone who's entirely reasonable. He can't do it until he's ground himself down for ten years! Until then he has calculated on the basis of these principles a thousand times, and erected great constructions that are always correct down to the smallest detail; then he simply believes in them, the way a Catholic believes in revelation; it has always maintained itself with such fine solidity . . . so is there any trick involved in proving anything to such a person? On the contrary, no one could persuade him that his construction might well be standing, but the individual bricks vanish into thin air when you try to touch them!'

Törless felt disagreeably affected by Beineberg's exaggeration.

'It's probably not as bad as you imagine. I've never doubted that mathematics was right – that's what its success teaches us, after all – but I did think it was strange that it sometimes runs so contrary to the understanding; and perhaps it merely appears to do so.'

'Now, you can wait those ten years, maybe by then your understanding will have been properly prepared . . . But I've been thinking about it too since we last talked about it, and I'm quite convinced that there's a snag to it. And by the way, you used to talk about it quite differently from the way you do today.'

'Oh, no. I still think it's serious, but I don't want to exaggerate it as much as you do. I find the whole thing strange too. The idea of the irrational, of the imaginary, of lines that are parallel and intersect in infinity – somewhere or other – excites me. When I think about it I'm dazed, speechless.' Törless leaned forward, right into the shadow, and his voice was quietly muffled as he spoke. 'Before, everything was so clearly and distinctly ordered; but now it's as though my thoughts are like clouds, and when I come to particular points there's something like a hole in between and you can see through it into an infinite, indefinable expanse. Mathematics must be right; but what is it about my head, and what about all the others? Don't they feel it at all? How do they picture it? Not at all?'

'I think you could see it in your maths master. Look – if you happen upon something like that, you immediately look around and ask, how does that relate to everything else in me? *They've* drilled a path in a thousand curlicues through their brains, like the inside of a snail shell, and they can only see back as far as the next corner, whether the thread they're spinning behind them still holds or not. That's why you confuse them with your questions. None of them can find his way back. How can you say, by the way, that I'm exaggerating? These grown-ups and clever people have completely spun themselves into a web, one stitch supporting the next, so that the whole miracle looks entirely natural; but no one knows where the first stitch is, the one that holds everything up.

'We two have never spoken so seriously about it before, one doesn't like to talk at length about such things, but now you can see the weakness of the vision with which people are satisfied to see the world. It's a deception, it's a trick, it's nonsense! Anaemia!

Because their understanding is only sufficient to come up with their scientific explanation out of their own heads, but once outside the head it freezes to death, do you see? Ha ha! All of those points, those extremities that our teachers tell us are so delicate that we can't touch them yet, are dead – frozen – do you understand? Those much-admired points of ice are freezing all around us, and they're so lifeless that no one can do a thing with them!'

Törless had been leaning back for some time. Beineberg's hot breath was caught by the coats and warmed the corner. But as he always did when he was excited, Beineberg embarrassed Törless. Even now, as he leaned forward again, so close that his eyes were motionless before Törless, like two greenish stones, while his hands jerked back and forth in the semi-darkness with a curiously ugly rapidity.

'All their claims are uncertain. Everything happens quite natur-ally, they say – if a stone falls, that's gravity, but why shouldn't it be the will of God, and why shouldn't someone who feels like it be released from sharing the fate of the stone? But what am I doing talking to you about such things? You'll only ever be half-way there! Finding something a bit strange, shaking your head a bit, being a bit shocked – that's your way; you don't dare go beyond it. That, incidentally, isn't to my disadvantage.'

'But it is to mine? Your assertions aren't all that certain, either.'

'How can you say that! They're the only certainties. Why should I quarrel with you over it? You'll see, my dear Törless; I'd even be willing to bet that you'll be incredibly interested in the explanation we find for them. For example, when we get Basini where we –'

'Please, that's enough,' Törless interrupted him, 'I don't want to get involved with that right now.'

'Oh, why not?'

'I just don't. I don't like it. Basini and the other thing are two different things for me; and I don't usually cook two things in the same pot.'

Beineberg twisted his mouth at this unfamiliar resoluteness, even brutality, on the part of his younger schoolmate. But Törless felt that the mere fact of naming Basini had undermined his whole certainty, and he spoke in annoyance to hide that. 'You are asserting things with a certainty that is almost crazy. Don't you think your theories might be built on sand just like the others? The curlicues in your brain are even more stubborn and obscure than the ones you were just describing, and they presuppose much more goodwill on the listener's part.'

Curiously, Beineberg didn't become angry; he only smiled – although his smile was a little twisted, and his eyes sparkled with twice as much unease – and went on at once, 'You'll see, you'll see.'

'What will I see? And, my God, I'll just see; but I'm really not that interested, Beineberg! You don't understand me. You have no idea what interests me. If mathematics torments me, and if –' but he thought about it quickly and said nothing about Basini, 'if mathematics torments me, you and I are looking for completely different things behind it. I'm not looking for anything supernatural, it's the natural that I'm looking for – do you understand? Nothing outside of myself – I'm looking for something ... within myself! Something natural! But something I still don't understand! But you don't feel that any more than that maths chap does ... oh, just lay off me with your speculation for a while!'

Törless was trembling with excitement when he stood up.

And immediately Beineberg repeated, 'Well, we'll see, we'll see ...'

When Törless lay in bed that evening he couldn't get to sleep. The quarter-hours crept from his bed like nurses, his feet were icy cold, and the covers pressed down on him rather than keeping him warm.

The only sound in the dormitory was the quiet and even breathing of the pupils, who, after the hard work of lessons, gymnastics and running in the open air, had found healthy, animal sleep.

Törless listened to the breath of the sleeping boys. That was

Beineberg's breath, that was Reiting's, that Basini's; which? He didn't know; but one of the many, all even, peaceful, secure, rising and sinking like a great machine.

One of the linen curtains had only rolled down to half-height; beneath it the bright night gleamed in and drew a pale, motionless rectangle on the floor. The string had got stuck at the top or else had broken and hung down in ugly twists, while its shadow on the floor crept through the bright rectangle like a worm.

It all had a worrying, grotesque ugliness.

Törless tried to think of something pleasant. Beineberg occurred to him. Hadn't he trumped him today? Given his superiority a knock? Hadn't he, for the first time today, managed to preserve his unusual quality in the face of Beineberg? Emphasize it in such a way that Beineberg could feel the infinite difference in the delicacy of their sensibilities, which divided their two perceptions from one another? Did he have a ready reply? Yes or no? . . .

But that 'yes or no?' swelled in his head like rising bubbles and burst, and 'yes or no? . . . yes or no?' continued to swell repeatedly, unstoppably, in a stamping rhythm like the rolling of a railway train, like the nodding of flowers on stems too high for them, like the knocking of a hammer heard through many thin walls in a quiet house . . . That insistent, complacent 'yes or no?' offended Törless. His joy was inauthentic, it hopped about so ridiculously.

And finally, when he started awake, it seemed to be his own head nodding there, lolling on his shoulders, or bouncing up and down to the beat . . .

Finally everything within Törless fell silent. Before his eyes there was nothing but a broad, black patch that extended in a circle in all directions.

Then . . . from far away at the rim . . . two small, unsteady figures . . . came diagonally across the table. They were obviously his parents. But so small that he could feel nothing for them.

They disappeared again on the other side.

Then came two more; – but look, there was one walking backwards past them – taking steps twice the length of his body, – and already he had disappeared behind the rim; hadn't that been Beineberg? – Now those two: hadn't one of them been the maths master? Törless recognized him by the handkerchief sticking coquettishly out of his pocket. But who was the other one? The one with the very, very fat book under his arm, which was half as tall as he was himself? Who could barely stand up, it was so heavy? ... With each step they stopped and put the book on the ground. And Törless heard the squeaky voice of his teacher saying: 'If that's how he thinks it is, the correct answer is to be found on page twelve, page twelve refers us on to page fifty-two, but then what we find on page thirty-one is also true, with this precondition ...' And they bent over the book and reached into it with their hands, sending the pages flying. After a while they stood up again, and the other man stroked the teacher's cheeks five or six times. Then they stepped forwards a few paces, and once again Törless heard the voice, as though it was counting off an endless mathematical proof. Until the other man stroked the maths master again.

That other man ... ? Törless frowned to see better. Wasn't he wearing a periwig? And rather old-fashioned clothes? Very old-fashioned indeed? Even silk knee breeches? Wasn't it ... ? Oh! And Törless awoke with a cry: Kant!

The next moment he smiled; the room around him was very peaceful, the breathing of the sleeping boys had grown quiet. He had been asleep, too. And by now his bed was warm again. He stretched himself comfortably out under the covers.

'So I've been dreaming about Kant,' he thought. 'Why didn't it last longer? He might have had a chat with me.' And he did remember how once, when he had been unprepared for history class, he had spent all night dreaming so vividly about the people and events concerned that the next day he was able to talk about them as though he had been there, and got an excellent mark in the exam. And now, once again, he thought of Beineberg, Beineberg and Kant – the conversation he had had the previous day.

Slowly the dream retreated from Törless – as slowly as a silk sheet endlessly sliding down the skin of a naked body.

But his smile soon made way for a strange unease. Had his thoughts advanced by one single step? Could he glean *anything* from this book which would contain the solution to all mysteries? And his victory? Certainly, it had been only his unexpected animation that had made Beineberg fall silent . . .

Again he was overwhelmed by a profound feeling of listlessness and physical disgust. He lay there for several minutes, hollowed out with nausea.

But then, all of a sudden, he became aware of the sensation that his body was touched at every point by the mild, lukewarm canvas of the bed. Cautiously, very slowly and cautiously, Törless turned his head. That's right, there was the pale rectangle still on the stone floor – its sides slightly distorted, sure enough, but with that twisting shadow still creeping through it. He felt as though some danger lay in chains there, one that he could watch from his bed with a calm feeling of safety, as though protected by the bars of a cage.

In his skin, all over his body, a feeling awoke that suddenly turned into a remembered image. When he had been very small – yes, yes, that was it – when he had still worn little dresses and before he went to school, there were times when he felt a quite inexpressible longing to be a girl. And that longing wasn't in his head – oh no – and it wasn't in his heart – it tingled throughout his whole body and ran all over his skin. Yes, there were times when he felt so vividly like a girl that he thought he must really be one. Because in those days he knew nothing of the meaning of physical differences, and he couldn't understand why everyone kept telling him that he had to remain a boy for ever. And when he was asked why he thought he would rather be a girl, he had felt that there was no way of expressing it . . .

Today for the first time he felt something similar. Again, all around him, beneath his skin.

Something that seemed to be at once body and soul. Something rushing and hurrying, beating against his body as though with the velvety antennae of butterflies. And at the same time there was that defiant way that little girls have, of running away when they feel that grown-ups don't understand them, the arrogance with which they then giggle about the grown-ups, that terrible arrogance, always poised to dash off, as though it could at any moment retreat into some terribly deep hiding place in the little body . . .

Törless laughed quietly to himself, and again he stretched out comfortably along the covers.

That plump little manikin he had dreamed about, how greedily it had chased the pages beneath its fingers. And that rectangle down there? Ha, ha. Have clever little manikins ever noticed such a thing in their lives? He felt boundlessly protected against those clever people, and he felt for the first time that there was something in his sensuality – because he had known for ages that that was what it was – that no one could take from him, that no one could even copy, something that protected him against any form of alien cleverness like a very high, a very hidden wall.

'Had such clever little manikins ever in their lives,' he thought, taking the idea further, 'lain beneath a lonely wall and been startled by every trickle behind the mortar, as though something dead was trying to find the words to talk to them? Had they ever felt the music that the wind stirs up in the autumn leaves – felt to the very core that something terrifying suddenly lurked behind it . . . something that was slowly, slowly transforming itself into sensuality? But into such a strange sensuality, something more like flight and then like mocking laughter. Oh, it's easy to be clever if you aren't aware of all those questions . . .'

But again and again, in the meantime, the little mannikin seemed by stages to be growing into a giant, with a pitilessly stern expression, and each time it did so something like an electric shock twitched painfully out of Törless's brain and ran through his body. All that pain at still being made to stand outside a locked door – the very thing which had, a moment before, been swept away by the warm pulse of his blood – reawakened, and a wordless lament flowed through Törless's soul, like the howling of a dog quivering over wide fields at night.

So he fell asleep. A few times, in his half-sleep, he looked over to the patch by the window, as one might mechanically reach for a supporting rope to feel whether it was still stretched taut. Then there loomed indistinctly in his mind the resolution that the next morning he would think very carefully about himself – ideally with pen and paper – and then, right at the end, there was only pleasant, tepid warmth – like a bath and a sensual stirring – which, although he was not at all aware of it being so, was in some entirely unrecognizable but very emphatic way associated with Basini.

Then he fell into a deep and dreamless sleep.

And yet that was his first thought when he woke up the next day. Now he would have been very glad to know what it really was, since he had been half thinking and half dreaming about Basini towards the end, but he wasn't capable of remembering that.

So all that remained was a mood of tenderness, like that which prevails in a house at Christmas when the children know the presents are there, but still locked up behind the mysterious door, and all that can be seen, here and there, is a glint of light through the cracks.

In the evening Törless stayed in the classroom; Beineberg and Reiting had disappeared off somewhere, probably to the attic hideaway; Basini sat in his seat at the front, hunched over a book with his head resting on his hands.

Törless had bought himself a notebook, and carefully arranged his pen and ink. Then he wrote on the first page, after some hesitation: *De natura hominum.* He thought he owed the philosophical subject-matter a Latin title. Then he drew a large, artistic flourish around the heading and leaned back in his chair to wait for it to dry.

But it had dried long since, and he had still not picked up his pen again. Something kept him fixed motionless to the spot. It was the hypnotic atmosphere of the big, hot lamps, the animal warmth emanating from that mass of people. He had always been receptive to that state, which could intensify to a feverish physical feeling that was always connected with an extraordinary level of mental sensitivity. And the same was true today. In the course of the day he had worked out what he actually wanted to write down; that whole series of experiences, from the evening at Božena's to the indistinct sensuality that had recently come upon him. If it was all set down in an orderly fashion, one fact after another, he hoped that the correct, intellectually legitimate version would yield itself of its own accord, just as an outline emerges from the confusion of a hundred intersecting curves. And he wanted nothing more than that. But so far he had felt like a fisherman who might be able to tell from a twitching on his net that a heavy prey has fallen into his trap, but for all his efforts is unable to haul it into the light.

And now Törless did begin to write – but hastily, with no attention to form. 'I feel,' he wrote, 'something within me, and don't really know what it is.' But then he quickly crossed the line out and wrote in its place: 'I must be ill – insane!' A shudder ran through him, because the word felt agreeably dramatic. 'Insane – or what else could it be, when things that seem quite normal to other people seem so strange to me? That this strangeness should torment me? That it inspires lewd' – he deliberately chose that word, with its connotations of biblical unction, because it seemed darker and more freighted with meaning – 'feelings in me? I have faced this before, like all young men, like all my classmates . . .' But here he came to a standstill. 'Isn't that true?' he thought to himself. 'At Božena's, for example, that was so peculiar; so when did it actually begin? . . . Anyway,' he thought, 'it did at some point.' But he left the sentence unfinished.

'What are the things that seem strange to me? The most trivial. Mostly inanimate objects. What is it that seems strange about them? Something that's new to me. But that's exactly it! Where do I get that "something" from? I feel its existence; it has an effect on me; as though it wanted to speak. I am as over-excited as someone who is supposed to be able to lip-read a paralysed man's words from the distortions of his mouth, and is unable to do it. It's as though I have a greater aptitude than other people, but one that is not fully developed, an aptitude that exists, that makes its presence felt, but doesn't work. The world for me is full of silent voices: so am I a clairvoyant, or am I prone to hallucinations?

'But it isn't only inanimate objects that have an effect on me. No, what increases my doubt is that it's people, too. Up until a certain point in time I see them as they see themselves. Beineberg and Reiting, for example – they have their storeroom, a perfectly normal attic hideaway, because they like having somewhere they can retreat to. They do one thing because they're furious with one boy, and something else because they want to prevent another boy from swaying their schoolmates. Perfectly clear and comprehensible reasons. But today they sometimes appear as though I'm dreaming and they're characters in my dream. Not their words, not just their actions, no, sometimes everything about them, if they are physically near, has the same effect on me as inanimate objects do. And yet I hear them speaking just as they did before, I can see that their actions and words fall under exactly the same categories ... I'm forever sensing that nothing extraordinary is taking place, and at the same time something within me is forever protesting that it can't be so. This change began, if I remember correctly, with Basini's ...'

Here Törless glanced involuntarily over at Basini.

Basini was still sitting hunched over his book and appeared to be memorizing something. Seeing him sitting there like that, Törless's thoughts fell silent, and once again he could feel the effects of the seductive torments he had just described. For just as he noticed how quietly and innocuously Basini was sitting in front of him, in no way distinguished from the boys on either side of him, the humiliations that Basini had undergone sprang to life in his mind. He did not think, with the affability that comes with moral reflection, of telling himself that after suffering a humiliation every human being has the potential at least to try to appear casual and confident as quickly as possible. Rather, something immediately stirred in him with a terrible whirling motion like a spinning-top, momentarily bending Basini's image into the most incredible contortions, then tearing it apart into the most unimaginably dislocated postures, so that he himself grew dizzy. But these were only comparisons that he came up with in retrospect. During that moment he had only the feeling that something within him was whirling up like a crazily spinning top from his tightened chest to his head, the feeling of his dizziness. Into the midst of that, like sparks, like coloured dots, leapt feelings that Basini had on various occasions inspired in him.

In fact the feeling had always been one and the same. And more precisely it was not a feeling at all, more of an earthquake deep within the core of him, which caused no perceptible waves and which none the less made the whole of his soul tremble with such restrained power that the waves of even the stormiest feelings seemed in comparison harmless ripples on the surface.

If that single feeling had seemed different to him on different occasions, it was because, whenever he wished to interpret those waves that flooded through the whole of his being, all that reached his consciousness was a series of images. It was as though all that could be seen of a swell stretching endlessly into the darkness was individual particles spraying up against the rocks of an illuminated shore, before falling back exhausted out of the circle of light.

So these impressions were unstable, changing, accompanied by an awareness of their arbitrary nature. Törless could never keep them still, because each time he looked more closely he felt that these surface phenomena bore no relation to the weight of the dark mass below, which they seemed to represent.

He never 'saw' Basini in any vivid, plastic physical attitude, he never had a real vision. It was only ever the illusion of one, a vision of his visions. For he always felt as though an image had just flashed across the mysterious surface, and he never managed to catch it as it was actually happening. So he was always filled with a restless unease, such as that which one feels watching a cinematic film when, despite the illusion of the whole, one is unable to shake off a vague perception that behind the image which one receives hundreds of different images are flashing by, each quite different when seen individually.

But he didn't know where to look within himself for that power to create an illusion – a power which always fell short, by an immeasurably small degree, of being quite strong enough. He was only dimly aware that it had something to do with that mysterious quality his soul had of being pounced upon by inanimate objects, mere things, as though by a hundred silent, questioning eyes.

So Törless sat very still, rigid, forever glancing across towards Basini, entirely engrossed in the mad whirl within him. And again and again a single question arose: What is that special quality that I have? As time passed he could no longer see Basini, nor the hot, glowing lamps, nor did he feel the animal warmth all around, nor the humming roar that rises from a crowd of people, even if they are only whispering. Like a hot, darkly glowing mass it all emitted an undifferentiated vibration in a circle around him. Only in his ears did he feel a burning sensation, and an icy cold in his fingertips. He was in that state more of mental than of physical fever which he so loved. That atmosphere grew more and more intense, mingled with impulses of tenderness. In the past, when he was in that state, he had liked to devote himself to memories. And that same languid warmth awoke in him now. There it was: a memory ... He had been travelling ... in a little Italian town ... he was staying with his parents in an inn not far from the theatre. Every evening they performed the same opera in that town, and every evening he heard every word, every note wafting across to him. He did not know the language. And yet each evening he sat by the open window and listened. In this way he fell in love with one of the actresses, although he had never seen her. The theatre had never again moved him as it did in those days; he felt the passion in the melodies like the wing beats of great dark birds, as though he could follow the lines that their flight drew in his soul. What he heard were no longer human passions, no, these were passions that had escaped from human beings, as though from cramped and ordinary cages. In his excitement he could never think of the people over there who were – invisibly – acting out his passions; whenever he tried to imagine them, at that moment dark flames shot up before his eyes, or unimaginably gigantic dimensions appeared before him, just as in darkness human bodies grow and human eyes gleam like the reflections of the deepest wells. In those days he had loved those dark flames, those eyes in the dark, those dark wing beats, he had loved them under the name of that actress of whom he knew nothing.

And who had written the opera? He had no idea. Perhaps it was based on a trite, sentimental love story. Had its creator ever felt that the music would transform it into something else?

One thought concentrated Törless's whole body. Are adults like that, too? Is the world like that? Is it a universal law that there is something within us that is stronger, bigger, more beautiful, more passionate, darker than we are ourselves? Something over which we are so powerless that we can only aimlessly scatter a thousand seeds until suddenly one of them sprouts forth like a dark flame that finally towers over us? . . . And every nerve in his body quivered with the impatient answer: Yes.

Törless looked around, eyes gleaming. The lamps, the warmth, the light, the industrious boys were still there. But in the midst of all this he felt as though he had been chosen. He felt like a saint who has heavenly visions – because he knew nothing of the intuition of the great artists.

Hurriedly, with the speed of fear, he reached for his pen and jotted down a few lines about his discovery; once again, something like a light seemed to burst forth within him – then an ash-grey rain broke over his eyes, and the brilliance within his spirit was extinguished.

But the episode with Kant was by now almost entirely over and done with. By day Törless no longer gave it a thought; he was too vividly convinced that he himself was close to solving his riddles to give a thought to how anyone else might go about it. Since the previous evening he had felt as though the handle to the door into that further place had been in his hand, and had slipped away from him once more. But having seen that he must do without the help of philosophy books, and having no real trust in them, he had no idea how he would be able to clutch that handle once again. He made a few attempts to take his notes further, but the written words remained dead, a series of sullen, long-familiar question marks, and the moment in which he had seen through them into a vault lit by quivering candle flames would not be reawakened.

So he resolved to seek out, time and again and as often as possible, the situations that held that curious significance for him; and his eye came to rest with particular frequency upon Basini, when the boy, thinking himself unobserved, walked innocently among the others. 'At some point,' Törless thought to himself, 'it will come back to life, and then perhaps it will be more intense and clear than it was before.' And he was greatly calmed by the thought that where such matters were concerned one was in a dark room, and that when one's fingers had lost their place the only thing to do was to go on fumbling randomly, again and again, along the dark wall.

But at night this thought grew rather faint. Then Törless felt rather ashamed that he had passed over his original resolution to look in the book his teacher had shown him for the explanation that it might contain. Then he lay there quietly and listened across to Basini, whose violated body breathed peacefully like all the others. He lay quietly, like a huntsman in his hide, feeling that he was biding his time and his reward would surely come. But just as the idea of the book had sprung to mind, a fine-toothed doubt gnawed away at his tranquillity, a sense that he was wasting his time, a hesitant admission that he had suffered a defeat.

As soon as that vague feeling asserted itself, his attention lost the comfortable feeling that comes from watching the progress of a scientific experiment. Then Basini seemed to exude a physical influence, a fascination, like that which comes when one is sleeping near a woman and could at any moment pull the covers from her. A tingle in the brain prompted by the awareness that one need only stretch out one's hand, the same thing that often drives young couples to engage in debaucheries that far exceed their sensual needs.

According to the intensity of the reflection that his endeavours might strike him as ludicrous if he knew everything that Kant knew, everything that his mathematics master or anyone who had completed his studies knew – according to the intensity of that emotional shock, his sensual urges grew weaker or stronger, keeping his eyes hot and open despite the general silence as everyone around him slept. Indeed, sometimes those urges blazed up in him so powerfully that they suffocated all other thoughts. At such times, he yielded, half willingly, half desperately, to their temptations. As he did so he felt only what is felt by all of those people who never incline to a crazed and debauched sensuality, one that tears the soul apart, tears it apart with voluptuous purpose, so much as they do when they have suffered a failure that has shaken the balance of their self-confidence.

Then, after midnight, as he quietly drifted into unquiet sleep, he thought he was aware of someone from the area around Reiting's or Beineberg's bed picking up his coat and walking over to Basini. Then he thought he heard them leaving the dormitory ... But it could equally well have been his imagination.

Two holidays were coming up; as they fell on a Monday and a Tuesday, the headmaster gave the pupils the Saturday off, and they had four days' holiday. For Törless, however, this was not enough time to make the long journey home, so he had hoped at least that his parents would visit him, but urgent business kept his father in the ministry, and his mother was unwell, and did not feel up to the exertions of the journey on her own.

Only when Törless received the letter in which his parents told him they were not coming, adding many tender consolations, did he feel happy with the arrangement. He would almost have thought it disruptive – at least it would have confused him terribly – to have had to face his parents at that moment.

Many pupils received invitations to nearby estates. Even Jusch, whose parents had a lovely farm a day's journey from the little town, took a holiday, and Beineberg, Reiting and Hofmeier went with him. Jusch had also invited Basini, but Reiting had ordered him to turn down the invitation. Törless claimed not to know whether his parents were coming or not; he didn't feel at all in the mood for innocently cheerful festivities and entertainments.

By Saturday afternoon the great building was silent and almost deserted.

When Törless walked along the corridors, they echoed from one end to the other; no one paid him any attention, because most of the teachers had gone away, on a shooting-party or somewhere else. It was only over meals, now served in a small room near the deserted refectory, that the few remaining pupils saw one another. Leaving the table, they dispersed once more among the various corridors and rooms, and the silence of the building swallowed them up. In between they led a life to which no one paid any more attention than they did to the spiders and millipedes in the cellar and the attic.

Apart from a few boys in the sickbay, the only members of Törless's class who had stayed behind were himself and Basini. When they were saying their goodbyes, Törless and Reiting had exchanged some furtive words on the subject of Basini. Reiting was worried that Basini might use the opportunity to seek protection from one of the teachers, and he particularly asked Törless to keep a close eye on him.

But Törless's attention would have been focused on Basini anyway.

The hubbub of arriving cars, of servants carrying cases, the jocular farewells of the pupils leaving the school, had barely passed before the awareness of being alone with Basini took overwhelming possession of Törless.

That was after the first midday meal. Basini was sitting at his desk at the front of the room, writing a letter. Törless had sat down in a corner at the very back, and was trying to read.

It was the first time that Törless had returned to his volume of Kant, and he had carefully planned the situation so that it would be like this. Basini was sitting at the front, Törless was sitting at the back, with his eyes fixed on him, boring through him. And this was how he planned to read, immersing himself further in Basini after each page. This was the way; this was how he had to find the truth, without losing his grip on life, living, complicated, ambiguous life . . .

But it didn't work, as always, when he thought something through too carefully in advance. It wasn't spontaneous enough, and his mood soon lapsed into a stubborn, gluey boredom that clung to each of his repeated and over-deliberate efforts.

Törless furiously threw the book on the floor. Basini looked around with a start, but then immediately went on hastily writing.

The hours crept on like this towards dusk. Törless sat there befuddled. The only thing to reach his consciousness, out of a general dull, whirring, droning sensation, was the ticking of his pocket-watch. It wagged along behind the lethargic body of the hours like a little tail. The room became blurred . . . Surely Basini couldn't still be writing . . . 'Ah, he probably doesn't dare turn on the light,' Törless thought to himself. But was he still in his seat? Törless had been gazing out into the bare, gloomy landscape and had to accustom his eyes to the darkness of the room. Yes, there, that motionless shadow, that'll be him. Listen, he's even sighing – once, twice . . . Or is he asleep?

A servant came and lit the lamps. Basini started awake and rubbed his eyes. Then he took a book from his desk and looked as though he was trying to memorize something.

Törless's lips burned to speak to him, and to avoid doing so he quickly left the room.

That night Törless came close to attacking Basini, such a murderous sensuality had awoken in him after the pain of the unthinking, dull-witted day. Fortunately sleep rescued him in time.

The next day passed, bringing nothing but the same barren quietness. The silence and expectancy left Törless overwrought – the constant attentiveness consumed all his mental powers, leaving him incapable of thought.

Crushed, disappointed, so dissatisfied with himself that he was prone to the most awful doubts, he went to bed early.

He had been lying for a long time in restless, feverish half-sleep, when he heard Basini coming.

Without stirring, he gazed after the dark figure walking past his bed; he heard the sound of clothes being undone; then the rustling of the covers being drawn over the body.

Törless held his breath, but he could hear nothing more. And yet he couldn't shake off the feeling that Basini wasn't sleeping, but listening just as hard to the darkness as he was.

Quarter-hours passed – hours. Interrupted here and there by the quiet sound of bodies stirring quietly in bed.

Törless was in a curious state that kept him awake. Yesterday his fever had been caused by sensual images in his imagination. Only right at the end had they taken a turn towards Basini. Under the relentless hand of sleep, which erased them, they had rebelled for one last time, and he had only a very dim memory of that. Today, though, from the start, there had been nothing but a compulsive desire to get up and walk over to Basini. It had been hardly bearable while he had had the feeling that Basini was awake and listening out for him. And only now, when Basini was probably asleep, was there a cruel thrill in the idea of falling on the sleeping boy as one might fall on one's prey.

Törless already felt the movements of sitting up and getting out of bed twitching in all his muscles. But none the less he could not yet shake off his immobility.

'What would I do with him?' he wondered in his fear, almost out loud. And he had to admit that his cruelty and sensuality had no real object. He would have been confused if he actually had jumped on Basini. Surely he didn't want to beat him up? God forbid! So how did he plan on using Basini to satisfy his sensual impulses? He felt an involuntary repulsion when he thought of the various vices to which young boys are prone. Laying himself bare like that before another human being? Never! . . .

But as that revulsion grew, the impulse to walk over to Basini intensified as well. Finally Törless was utterly convinced of the senselessness of any such endeavour, but a physical compulsion seemed to pull him from bed as though he was tied to a rope. And while all the images fled from his mind and he kept saying to himself that it would probably be best to try and go to sleep now, he rose mechanically from his bed. Very slowly – feeling that the mental compulsion was painstakingly gaining ground against the resistance it encountered – he got up. First one arm . . . then he drew up his torso, then pushed one knee out from under the blanket . . . then . . . and then all at once he dashed barefoot on tiptoe over to Basini, and sat down on the edge of the bed.

Basini was asleep.

He looked as though he was having pleasant dreams.

Törless was not yet master of his actions. For a moment he sat quietly and stared into the sleeping boy's face. Twitching through his brain were those short, disconnected thoughts which do no more than record the state of things, the thoughts that one has when one loses one's balance or falls, or when an object is torn from one's hands. And without thinking he grabbed Basini by the shoulder and shook him awake.

The sleeping boy stretched lethargically a few times, then sat up and looked at Törless, his eyes stupid with sleep.

Törless was frightened; he was utterly confused; for the first time he became aware of what he was doing, and didn't know what to do next. He was terribly ashamed. His heart beat audibly. Words of explanation, excuses jostled on his tongue. He wanted to ask Basini if he had any matches, if he could tell him what time it was . . .

Basini continued to stare at him uncomprehendingly.

Now, without having uttered a word, Törless drew back his arm, now he was sliding down from the bed to creep silently back to his own – then Basini seemed to have grasped the situation and sat upright with a jolt.

Törless stood irresolutely at the end of the bed. Basini looked at him again with a questioning, inquiring glance, then he rose from his bed, slipped into his dressing-gown and slippers and padded on ahead.

All of a sudden Törless knew that it wasn't the first time this had happened.

In passing he picked up the keys to the room, which he had hidden under his pillow. Basini made straight for the attic hideaway. He seemed to have become very familiar with the path which had once been kept secret from him. He held the crate firmly when Törless stepped on to it, he pushed the stage sets aside, warily, discreetly, like a trained lackey.

Törless opened the door and they stepped inside. He stood with his back to Basini and lit the little lamp.

When he turned around, Basini was standing naked before him.

He involuntarily took a step back. He was blinded and appalled by the sudden sight of that naked, snow-white body, with the red of the walls turning to blood behind him. Basini had a beautiful physique; his body, almost entirely lacking in masculine forms, was as chastely slender as that of a young girl. And Törless felt the image of that nakedness lighting up in his nerves like hot, white flames. He could not escape the power of that beauty. He had never known before what beauty was. For what was art, at his age, what did he know of it? Up to a certain age, after all, it is incomprehensible and boring to anyone who has grown up in the open air!

But now it had come to him along the paths of sensuality. Covertly, ambushing him. A stupefying warm breath emanated from the bared body, a soft, lascivious flattery. And yet there was something about it so solemn and compelling that it would have made one clasp one's hands together.

But after the initial surprise Törless was ashamed of both reactions. 'This is a man!' The thought infuriated him, and yet he felt as though he would have felt exactly the same way with a girl.

Ashamed, he said imperiously, 'What can you be thinking of? Get those things right back on . . . !'

Now it was Basini's turn to seem dismayed; hesitantly, without taking his eyes off Törless, he picked up his dressing-gown.

'Go on, sit down!' Törless ordered. Basini obeyed. Törless leaned against the wall, hands crossed behind his back.

'Why did you get undressed? What did you want from me?'

'I thought . . .'

Hesitation.

'What did you think?'

'The others . . .'

'What about the others?'

'Beineberg and Reiting . . .'

'What about Beineberg and Reiting? What have they been doing? You've got to tell me everything! That's what I want; do you understand? Although I've already heard it from the lips of the others.' Törless blushed at his clumsy lie. Basini bit his lips.

'Now, all right?'

'No, don't make me tell you! Please don't ask me to do that! I'll do anything you like. But don't make me tell . . . Oh, you have such a special way of tormenting me ... !' Hatred, fear and a plea for mercy battled in Basini's eyes. Involuntarily Törless yielded.

'I don't want to torture you. I just want to force you to tell the whole truth yourself. Perhaps in your own interest.'

'But I haven't done anything particularly worth telling.'

'Really? So why did you take your clothes off?'

'They told me to.'

'And why did you do what they demanded of you? Are you a coward? A pitiful coward?'

'No, I'm not a coward! Don't say that!'

'Shut your mouth! If it's their beatings you're afraid of, let's see how mine suit you!'

'It's not their beatings I'm afraid of.'

'What are you afraid of, then?'

Törless was speaking calmly again. He was already annoyed by his crude threat. But it had slipped out against his will, just because he thought that Basini was taking more liberties with him than he did with the others.

'If you're not frightened, as you say, then what's wrong with you?'

'They tell me that if I do what they say everything will be forgiven after a while.'

'By the two of them?'

'No, in general.'

'How can they promise that? You've got me to think about as well!'

'They say they're going to take care of that.'

That gave Törless a shock. He remembered what Beineberg had said, that Reiting would deal with him just as he had with Basini. And if there really was a plot against him, what could he do to counter it? He was no match for them in that respect, and how far would they be able to go? Would they do what they had done with Basini? ... Everything in him rebelled at the malevolent notion.

Minutes passed between himself and Basini. He knew he lacked the daring and application for that kind of intrigue, but only because it didn't interest him sufficiently, because he never felt his entire personality was involved. He had always had more to lose than to gain. But if that ceased to be the case, he felt that he would have a quite different kind of toughness and courage. One only had to know when it was time to stake everything one had.

'Did they go into it in greater detail? About what they had in mind, where I was concerned?'

'No, they didn't. They just said they would take care of things.'

And yet . . . there was a danger . . . hiding somewhere . . . lying in wait for Törless . . . And with each step he might put his foot in a trap, each night might be the last before battle commenced. There was a terrible uncertainty in that idea. There was no more idle drifting, no more toying with mysterious tales. Things had hard corners now, tangible reality.

The conversation started up again.

'And what do they do to you?'

Basini said nothing.

'If you're serious about making things better, you have to tell me everything.'

'They make me get undressed.'

'Yes, yes, I've seen that . . . and then? . . .'

A few moments passed, and suddenly Basini said:

'Various things.'

He said it with a lascivious, womanly emphasis.

'So you're their . . . their mistress?'

'Oh no, I'm their friend!'

'How can you bring yourself to say that?'

'They say it themselves.'

'What . . . !'

'Yes, Reiting.'

'What do you mean, Reiting?'

'Yes, he's very kind to me. Usually I have to get undressed and read him something from history books; about Rome and its emperors, about the Borgias, about Tamberlaine . . . well, you know, all those great, bloody affairs. Then he can even be gentle with me.'

'And afterwards he usually beats me . . .'

'After what? . . . Oh, I see what you mean!'

'Yes. He says that if he didn't beat me he'd have to believe I was a man, and then he couldn't be so soft and gentle with me. But that way I belong to him, and he's not embarrassed.'

'And Beineberg?'

'Oh, Beineberg's frightful. Don't you think he has bad breath?'

'Shut up! It's no concern of yours what I think! Tell me what Beineberg does to you!'

'Well, the same as Reiting, but . . . But you're not to shout at me again –'

'Get on with it.'

'Just . . . in a different way. First he spends ages talking to me about my soul. He tells me I've sullied it, but only its outermost forecourt. Compared to the innermost soul it's something meaningless and external. But it has to be killed off. Many sinners have become saints by doing that. So in a higher respect sin isn't all that terrible; but you have to take it to its limit so that it breaks off. He makes me sit and stare at a piece of cut glass . . .'

'He hypnotizes you?'

'No, he says he just has to make all the things swimming around on the surface of my soul fall asleep and lose their power. Only then can he commune with my soul.'

'And how does he commune with it?'

'That experiment has never yet been successful. He sits there, and I have to lie down on the ground so that he can put his feet on my body. The glass must have made me very lethargic and sleepy. Then, all of a sudden, he orders me to bark. He describes it to me in detail: quietly, more of a whine, the way a dog barks in its sleep.'

'What's the point of that?'

'No idea. He also makes me grunt like a pig and tells me over and over again that there's something of the pig in me. But not as though he's insulting me; he repeats it to me quite quietly and kindly, to imprint it – that's what he says – firmly on to my nerves. Because he claims one of my former lives might have been a pig's, and that we have to entice it out to render it harmless.'

'And you believe all that?'

'Good God no; I don't think he believes it himself. And afterwards he's always quite different. How could I believe things of that kind? Who believes in the soul nowadays? Let alone the transmigration of souls? I know I've slipped up; but I've always hoped I'd be able to make amends. You don't need any hocus-pocus for that. I'm not going to rack my brains about why it was that I slipped up. Something like that happens so quickly, almost of its own accord. It's only afterwards that you realize you've done something stupid. But if he enjoys trying to find something supernatural in it, then I'm not going to stop him. But for the time being I must be at his beck and call. If only he'd stop pricking me . . .'

'What?'

'Yes, with a pin – not violently, just to see how I react . . . to see whether any part of my body reacts in a special way. But it does hurt. He claims that doctors don't know anything about it. I don't remember him saying what proof he has for that, I just remember him talking a lot about fakirs and how, when they see their souls, they're supposed to be insensitive to physical pain.'

'Yes, I know about those ideas; but you yourself said that that wasn't all.'

'Certainly not; but I did say I thought this was just a long-winded way of going about it. After that there are always long periods where he says nothing and I don't know what he's thinking about. But then he suddenly breaks off and demands that I perform services for him – like a man possessed – much worse than Reiting.'

'And you do everything he demands of you?'

'What other option have I? I want to be a respectable person again, and enjoy my peace and quiet.'

'But you don't care what's happened in the meantime?'

'There's nothing I can do about it.'

'Now listen carefully and answer my questions: how come you were capable of stealing?'

'How come? Look, I urgently needed the money; I owed money to the man in the tuck shop and he wasn't going to be fobbed off any longer. Then I was absolutely certain that some money was coming my way. None of my classmates would lend me any: some of them had none, and the thrifty ones are delighted when someone who isn't so good at saving is in trouble by the end of the month. I didn't want to cheat anyone; I just wanted to borrow the money secretly –'

'That's not what I mean.' Törless impatiently interrupted the story that was clearly bringing Basini some relief. 'I'm asking how come – how could you do that, how did you feel? What was going on inside you at that moment?'

'Well – nothing at all. It was just a moment, I didn't feel anything, I didn't think about anything, and all of a sudden it had simply happened.'

'But the first time with Reiting? When he demanded things of you for the first time? Do you understand . . . ?'

'Oh, it was certainly unpleasant, because everything was an order. And then . . . just imagine how many people do that kind of thing for fun, and no one knows anything about it. It's not so bad in comparison.'

'But you carried out the order. You humiliated yourself. As if you would be willing to crawl in the mud because someone else wanted you to.'

'I admit it. But I had to.'

'No, you didn't have to.'

'They'd have beaten me, they'd have reported me; all kinds of scandals would have landed on my head.'

'Fine, forget about that. I want to know something else from you. Listen, I know you've spent a lot of money at Božna's. You opened up to her, you bragged to her, you boasted of your manliness. So you want to be a man? Not just with your mouth and your . . . but with the whole of your soul? Look, all of a sudden someone asks you to perform a humiliating service like that, and the same moment you feel you're too cowardly to say no: didn't your whole being feel torn asunder? Wasn't there some vague terror, as though something unspeakable had happened inside you?'

'God, I don't understand you; I don't know what you're after; I can't say anything to you, anything at all.'

'Listen to me; now I'm going to order you to get undressed again.' Basini smiled.

'To lie flat on the ground in front of me. Don't laugh! I really am ordering you to do this! Do you hear! If you don't obey this minute, you'll see what's in store for you when Reiting comes back! . . . So. You see, you lie down naked on the ground in front of me. You're trembling; are you cold? I could spit on your naked body right now, if I wanted to. Press your head firmly down on the ground. Doesn't the dust on the floor look funny? Like a landscape full of clouds and rocks as big as houses? I could prick you with pins. There are some there in the corner, next to the lamp. Do you feel them on your skin? . . . But I don't want to do that. I could make you bark, like Beineberg did, I could make you eat dust like a pig, I could make you move in a particular way – you know – and you would have to sigh: "Oh, my dear mother" –'

But Törless suddenly broke off his sacrilege. 'But I don't want to, do you understand?'

Basini was crying. 'You're tormenting me.'

'Yes, I'm tormenting you. But that's not the important thing for me; I just want to know one thing: if I push all that into you like knives, what is inside you? What is happening inside you? Does something explode in you? Tell me! Suddenly, like a piece of glass that suddenly explodes into a thousand splinters before it's shown so much as a crack? The image you've made of yourself, isn't it extinguished by a breath? Doesn't another one leap to appear in its place, as magic-lantern pictures leap out of the darkness? Do you not understand me at all? I can't explain it any better than that; you have to tell me yourself . . . !'

Basini wept incessantly. His girlish shoulders shuddered; he was able only to say a single thing, over and over again: 'I don't know what you want; I can't explain anything to you. It happens on the spur of the moment; it can't happen any other way; you would do exactly the same as I do.'

Törless said nothing. He leaned against the wall, exhausted and motionless, staring straight ahead.

'If you were in my situation, you'd do exactly the same,' Basini had said. What had happened was presented as a simple necessity, peaceful and undistorted.

Törless's self-confidence revolted in sheer contempt against the mere presumption. And yet that rebellion by his entire being seemed to offer no satisfactory guarantee. '. . . Yes, I would have more character than he does, I wouldn't stand for such outrageous demands – but does any of it matter? Does it matter that I would act differently out of firmness, out of respectability, for reasons that are now quite irrelevant to me? No, what matters isn't how I would act, but the fact that if I really did act like Basini, I'd feel it was every bit as normal as he does. That's the important thing: my sense of myself would be just as straightforward, just as unambiguous as his . . .'

This thought – coming to him in scraps of sentences, superimposed on one another and constantly going back to the beginning – added to his contempt for Basini a very intimate pain, one which was quiet but which touched his innermost equilibrium more profoundly than any morality could do. It came from the memory of a sensation that had recently come to Törless, and which would not let go of him. When Basini had made him aware of the possible threat to himself from Reiting and Beineberg, he had been simply terrified. Simply terrified as though he had been ambushed, and without reflection he had rapidly sought a way of parrying the attack and covering himself. That had happened at a moment of real threat, and he was irritated by the sensation he had felt then. Those quick, thoughtless impulses. In vain he tried to unleash them once again. But he knew that they had within an instant taken away from the danger everything that was strange and ambiguous about it.

And yet it had been the same danger that he had sensed only a few weeks before, in the same place, when he had been so terrified by the storeroom which lay there like a forgotten corner of the Middle Ages, far from the warm, bright life of the classrooms, and by Beineberg and Reiting, because they seemed suddenly to have turned from the people they were down below, and to have become something quite different, something dark and bloodthirsty; characters from a quite different life. That had been a transformation, a leap for Törless, as though the image of his surroundings had suddenly appeared before different eyes, eyes that had awoken from a hundred years of sleep.

And yet the danger had been the same . . . He kept on repeating that to himself. And again and again he tried to compare the memories of the two different sensations . . .

Meanwhile Basini had been standing up for some time; he noticed his companion's fixed, absent gaze, quietly picked up his clothes and crept away.

Törless saw him – as if through a fog – but let him go without a word.

All his attention was consumed with the effort of rediscovering that point within himself where the transformation in his inner perspective had suddenly occurred.

But every time he approached it, he felt like someone trying to compare something close to him with something far away: he could never capture the remembered images of the two feelings at the same time, but each time, like a quiet click, there came a feeling that corresponded to something in the physical realm, those barely perceptible muscular sensations that accompany the focusing of the eye. And each time, precisely at the crucial moment, it claimed all his attention, the activity of comparison interposed itself before the object being compared, there was a barely noticeable twinge – and everything stood still.

And Törless would start again from the beginning.

This mechanically regular procedure lulled him into a rigid, waking, ice-cold sleep that kept him fixed motionlessly in his place, and for an indefinite length of time.

A thought woke Törless like the quiet touch of a warm hand. A thought so apparently obvious that he was amazed not to have hit upon it ages before.

A thought that did nothing but record the experience he had just had: anything that looks big and mysterious from afar always arrives as something simple and undistorted, in natural, everyday proportions. It is as though an invisible frontier has been drawn around each human being. Something that has been prepared else-where and which approaches from afar, is like a misty sea full of giant, changing forms; what approaches the person, becomes action, impacts against one's life, is small and distinct, with human dimensions and human features. And between the life that is lived and the life that is felt, sensed and seen from a long way off, that invisible frontier lies like a narrow door, through which the images of events must cram themselves together in order to enter the human being.

And yet, close as this was to his own experience, Törless reflectively lowered his head.

'A curious thought . . .' he felt.

Finally he was lying in his bed. He wasn't thinking about any-thing now, because thought was so difficult and so fruitless. What he had learned of his friends' secret intrigues ran through his mind, but as indifferently, as lifelessly as a news item read in a foreign newspaper.

There was nothing more to be hoped for from Basini. That was his problem, of course! But it was so uncertain, and he was so tired and so downcast. An illusion, perhaps – the whole thing.

Only the sight of Basini, of his naked, gleaming skin, was like a sprig of lilac scenting the twilit sensations that preceded sleep. Even all moral revulsion faded away. Finally Törless fell asleep.

No dream disturbed his rest. Only an infinitely agreeable warmth spread soft carpets beneath his body. Finally he woke up. And he almost screamed. Basini was sitting on the edge of his bed. And the next moment, with furious speed, Basini had stripped the nightshirt from his body and slipped under the covers, and was pressing his naked, quivering body against Törless.

As soon as Törless had recovered from the shock he pushed Basini away.

'What on earth are you thinking of . . . !'

But Basini pleaded. 'Oh, don't be like that again! There isn't anyone like you. They don't despise me like you do; they only pretend to, so that they can be different again afterwards. And you? You of all people . . . ? . . . You're even younger than I am, although you're stronger. We're both younger than the others . . . You're not as coarse and boastful as they are . . . you're gentle . . . I love you . . . !'

'What – what are you saying? What do you want from me? Go – go away!' And Törless, tormented, pressed his arm against Basini's shoulder. But the hot proximity of the soft, strange skin pursued and surrounded him, suffocating him. And all of a sudden Basini whispered . . .: 'Oh . . . do . . . please . . . oh, it would be a pleasure to serve you.'

Törless could think of no reply. While Basini was speaking, during the seconds of doubt and reflection, once more something like a deep, green sea had fallen over his senses. Only Basini's vivid words shone out in it, like the flashing of tiny, silver fish.

He still held his arms pressed against Basini's body. Something lay upon them like a moist, heavy warmth; their muscles slackened;

he forgot them . . . Only when some new, twitching word reached him did he wake up because he suddenly felt – like something terribly intangible – that just now, as in a dream, his hands had drawn Basini closer.

Then he wanted to shake himself awake, to shout at himself: Basini's tricking you; he only wants to pull you down to his level so that you can't despise him any more. But the cry stuck in his throat; no sound echoed through the spacious building; throughout all the corridors the dark tides of silence seemed motionless in sleep.

He wanted to find his way back to himself: but the tides lay outside all the doors like black wardens.

Then Törless stopped searching for words. The sensuality which had been gradually seeping into him from his isolated moments of despair had now reached its full extent. It lay naked beside him and covered his head with its soft black mantle. And it murmured sweet words of resignation into his ear and, with its warm fingers, it pushed away all questions and obligations as vain. And it whispered: 'In solitude everything is permitted.'

Only at the moment when he was carried away did he awaken for a second and clutch desperately at a single thought: 'This isn't me! ... isn't me! ... It won't be me again until tomorrow! ... Tomorrow ...'

On Tuesday evening the first pupils returned. Another batch was due to arrive later, on the night trains. There was constant hubbub in the building.

Törless was surly and jaded as he welcomed his friends; he had not forgotten. And then, too, they brought with them something so fresh and worldly from outside. It shamed him, since he had come to like the oppressive stuffiness of the narrow rooms.

He was often ashamed in general. Not just about what he had allowed himself to be seduced into – not such a rare thing in boarding-schools – but because he could now not help feeling a kind of tenderness for Basini, while at the same time feeling with greater urgency than ever how despised and humiliated the boy was.

He often had secret trysts with him. He led him to all the hiding places that he had learned about from Beineberg, and since Törless was not skilled at that kind of surreptitious creeping, Basini was soon able to find his way better than he could, and became his guide.

But at night a kind of jealousy, when he looked at Beineberg and Reiting, would not leave him in peace.

But they held back from Basini. Perhaps they were already bored with him. At any rate, a change seemed to have taken place within them. Beineberg was sinister and remote; when he spoke, it was to give mysterious hints of something to come. Reiting seemed to have turned his attention to other things; with his familiar skilfulness he wove the webs of various intrigues, trying to win over some boys by performing little favours for them, and frightening others by using furtive ploys to learn their secrets.

When they were all three together, Beineberg and Reiting insisted that it would soon be time to order Basini back to the storeroom or up to the attic.

Törless came up with all kinds of excuses to defer that moment, but his secret sympathy was a constant source of pain to him.

A few weeks previously he could not have imagined being in such a state, because he had inherited from his parents a powerful, healthy and natural constitution.

But it should not be imagined that Basini aroused any real desire in Törless, however fleeting and confused. Something like passion, certainly, had been roused in him, but love was certainly only an arbitrary, approximate name for it, and Basini the human being was no more than a substitute, a provisional object for that desire. For if Törless was debasing himself with Basini, his desire was never satisfied, but was growing beyond Basini and turning into a new, unspecific hunger.

*

At first he had been blinded only by the nakedness of the slender boy's body.

He had had the sense of being confronted with the forms of a very young girl, simply beautiful and far removed from anything sexual. It had been overwhelming, astonishing. And the purity that involuntarily emerged from that state had been that new and wonderfully uneasy feeling in his relationship towards Basini. But everything else had little to do with it. That surfeit of desire had existed for a long time – with Božena and long before that. It was the secret, unspecific, melancholy sensuality, free of any human object, of the maturing boy, which is like the damp, black, seed-bearing earth in the spring and like dark, subterranean waters that need only an arbitrary cause to rise and break their walls.

Törless's experiences had become that cause. A surprise, a misunderstanding, confused impressions, had smashed open the secret hiding places where everything furtive, forbidden, overheated, uncertain and lonely in Törless's soul had accumulated, and channelled those dark impulses towards Basini. Because there, all of a sudden, they encountered something which was warm, which breathed, which was fragrant, which was flesh, something that gave those indistinct and wandering dreams a form and part of its own beauty, in place of the corrosive ugliness with which Božena had tortured them in his loneliness. All at once a door to life was opened up for them, and everything mingled in the resulting half-light, desires and reality, orgiastic fantasies and impressions that still bore the warm traces of life, sensations that broke in from without and flames that flickered towards them from within, shrouding them beyond recognition.

For Törless himself, though, none of this could be distinguished any longer, and everything came together in a single, indistinct, unstructured feeling which he might, in his initial surprise, have taken for love.

*

But soon he learned to give a more accurate account of what had happened. From that point his unease drove him restlessly around. Hardly had he touched an object than he put it back down again. He could not hold a conversation with his classmates without falling silent for no reason, or distractedly changing the subject several times. Sometimes, in the middle of speaking, he would be overwhelmed by a wave of shame, and would blush, stammer and turn away . . .

He avoided Basini by day. If he could not avoid looking at him, he was almost always seized by disillusion. Every movement of Basini's filled him with nausea, the blurred shadows of his illusions were replaced by a cold, blunt brightness; his soul seemed to shrink until nothing remained of it but the memory of an earlier desire, which now seemed unutterably incomprehensible and repellent. He pressed his foot against the floor and hunched over himself, just to escape the pain of that shame.

He wondered what the others would say to him if they knew his secret, what his parents, his teachers would say.

But that final astonishment regularly brought his torments to an end. He was overwhelmed by a cool fatigue; with a pleasant shiver, his hot, slack skin became taut once more. Then he calmly let everyone pass by. But he was filled with a certain disdain for them all. He secretly suspected everyone he spoke to of the most terrible things.

And aside from that he thought he detected an absence of shame in them. He didn't think the others suffered as he knew he did. They seemed to lack the crown of thorns that his own pangs of conscience had placed upon his head.

But he felt like someone who had awoken from some profound agony. Like someone brushed by the hidden hands of disintegration. Like someone unable to forget the quiet wisdom of a lengthy illness.

He felt happy when he was in that state, and the moments when he longed for it returned again and again.

They began when he was able to look at Basini with indifference once again, and could endure his vile, repellent aspects with a smile. Then, while he knew that he was going to debase himself, he applied a new meaning to it. The uglier and more degrading what Basini offered him was, the greater was the contrast with the feeling of ailing refinement that set in later on.

Törless withdrew to some corner from which he was able to watch while remaining unseen. When he closed his eyes, he was filled with a vague sense of urgency, and when he opened them again he saw nothing to which it might relate. And then, all of a sudden, the thought of Basini grew vast and drew everything to itself. Soon it lost all definition. It seemed no longer to belong to Törless, and it seemed no longer to refer to Basini. It was surrounded by a whirl of emotions, as though by lascivious women in high-necked robes, with masks over their faces.

Törless knew none of them by name, nor did he know what any one of them concealed; but that was exactly where the intoxicating seductiveness lay. He no longer knew himself; and as a result his desire became a wild and contemptuous debauchery, as when, at some wanton party, the lights are suddenly extinguished and no one knows who it is that he is pulling to the ground and covering with kisses.

Later, once he had overcome the events of his youth, Törless became a young man with a very fine and sensitive mind. He became one of those aesthetic and intellectual characters upon whom respect for the law and, to some extent, for public morals, has a calming effect, relieving them of the need to think about anything coarse and remote from the finer things of the soul; but who, when asked to declare a more personal interest in the objects of morality and the law, bring to their grandiose outward show of correctness, with its hint of irony, a certain bored insensitivity. Because the interest which really does move them is focused solely upon the growth of their own soul, their own spirit or whatever we might choose to call that thing within us which is increased, now and then, by a thought between the words of a book or the sealed lips of a painting; that thing which sometimes awakens when some lonely, wilful melody drifts away from us and, as it disappears into the distance, tugs strangely at the thin scarlet thread of our blood which it trails behind it; but which has always vanished whenever we write up our files, manufacture machines, go to the circus or pursue a hundred similar occupations.

Such people, then, are extremely indifferent to any objects that challenge only their moral correctness. So, even later in life, Törless never felt any remorse for what had happened in those days. His needs had become so keenly and one-sidedly aesthetic that, had he been told a very similar tale of a lecher's debaucheries, it would never have occurred to him to voice his outrage at such behaviour. Such a person would have warranted his contempt not for being a lecher, but for being nothing better than that; not for his debaucheries, but for the state of mind that allowed him to commit them; because he was stupid or because his intelligence lacked any spiritual counterweights – always, in short, because of the sad, deprived and pathetic prospect that he presented. And, similarly, he would have despised him whether his vice had consisted in sexual debaucheries or in compulsive and degenerate drinking or cigarette-smoking.

And like everyone whose sole concern is the intensification of his mental abilities, the mere presence of torrid and excessive impulses meant little to him. He liked to think that the capacity for enjoyment, artistic talents, the highly refined spiritual life, was a piece of jewellery upon which one could easily injure oneself. He thought it inevitable that someone with a rich and active inner life would have certain moments about which other people could know nothing, and memories that he kept in secret drawers. And of such a person he asked only that he should know how to make refined use of those moments later in life.

And so, when someone to whom he had told the story of his youth asked him whether he was not sometimes ashamed of that memory, he gave the following reply with a smile: 'Of course I can't deny that it was degrading. Why would I? The degradation passed. But something of it lingered for ever: that tiny quantity of poison that is needed to rid the soul of its overly calm, complacent health, and instead to give it a kind of health that is more refined, acute and understanding.

'And would you wish to count the hours of degradation that are branded on the soul after any great passion? Just think of the hours of deliberate humiliation in love! Those enraptured hours that lovers spend leaning over certain deep wells, or placing their ears to one another's hearts, listening for the sound of the great, unsettled cats clawing against the dungeon walls? Just to feel themselves trembling! Just to fear being alone above those dark, fiery depths! Just suddenly – out of fear of their own loneliness with those dark forces – to seek refuge within one another!

'Just look into the eyes of young couples. "Do you really think . . . ?" they say. "But you have no idea how low we can sink!" – Those eyes contain a tranquil mockery of those who know nothing of so much, and the tender pride of those who have gone together through all kinds of hell.

'And just as these lovers go through these things together, in those days I went through them on my own.'

However, if that was Törless's judgement later on, in those days, when he was still caught up in the storm of his solitary longings, he had not yet attained that final confidence. All that remained of the mysteries that had lately been tormenting him was a vague echo, which sounded like a dark and distant note at the base of his experiences. He didn't want to think of that now.

But sometimes he had to. And when he did he was afflicted by a deep despair, and when he had those memories he was sometimes seized by a weary, hopeless shame.

And yet he was unable to account for that either.

This was because of the particular conditions that prevailed in the school. Here, where young, impulsive forces were imprisoned behind grey walls, the boys' imaginations were crammed full with random, voluptuous images that robbed more than one boy of his senses.

A certain degree of debauchery was even seen as manly, rakish, the bold grasping of forbidden pleasures – particularly if one compared oneself with the venerable and decrepit appearance of most of the teachers. Because if one did so, that exhortatory word 'morality' assumed a set of ludicrous associations with narrow shoulders, round bellies perched on thin legs and eyes that grazed as harmlessly as sheep behind their spectacles, as though life was nothing but a flowery field of solemn instruction.

In the school, in short, they had still no knowledge of life, no sense of all the gradations from coarseness and lechery to sickness and absurdity that fill the adult with revulsion when he hears of such things.

Törless lacked all those inhibitions, whose effectiveness we can only guess at. He had embarked upon his misdemeanours with the utmost naïvety.

For even the force of moral resistance, the spirit's capacity for sensitivity and feeling, which he was later to value so highly, was still absent. But there were signs that it was on its way. Törless was in error, he saw only the shadows cast in his consciousness by something as yet unrecognized, and he mistook them for reality: but he had to fulfil his duty to himself, a duty of the soul – even if he was still not up to such a task.

He knew only that he had been following something still un-defined along a path that led deep within him, and that it had left him exhausted. He had grown used to hoping for extraordinary, hidden discoveries, and in the process he had been led into the narrow, twisting chambers of sensuality. Not because he was per-verse, but because his spiritual situation was temporarily aimless.

And that very infidelity to something serious within him, some-thing for which he had striven, filled him with a vague sense of guilt; an indefinite, hidden nausea never quite left him, and a certain anxiety pursued him like someone running in the dark who no longer knows whether the path is still beneath his feet, or where he might have lost it.

Then he attempted to think of nothing at all. He went on living, mute and numb, forgetting all earlier questions. The refined enjoyment of his degradations became increasingly rare.

It did not yet leave him, but at the end of this time Törless put up no resistance when further decisions were made concerning Basini's future.

This happened some days later, when the three of them were together in the storeroom. Beineberg was very serious.

Reiting began to speak: 'Beineberg and I don't think we can keep on treating Basini as we have been doing. He's grown accustomed to the obedience he owes us, and it doesn't make him suffer any more; he's become cheeky and familiar, like a servant. So it's time to go a step further with him. Do you agree?'

'I don't yet know what you have in mind for him.'

'And it wouldn't be so easy to work it out. We must humiliate and oppress him still further. I'd like to see how far we can take it. How we go about it is another matter entirely. But I have some good ideas about that as well. We could, for example, give him a good thrashing, while he sang psalms of thanksgiving. That would be something to hear – each note covered over with gooseflesh. We could make him fetch us the filthiest things in his mouth, like a dog. We could take him to Božena's and read out his mother's letters, and Božena could supply amusing commentaries. But there's plenty of time for that. In the meantime we can quietly get on with producing new ideas, polishing them up and adding to them. It gets boring without the details. Perhaps we could just hand him over to the class. That would be the smartest thing to do. If everyone, and there are so many, contributes just a little, it's enough to tear him to pieces. I like these mass movements as a rule. No one intends to do anything in particular, and yet the waves grow ever higher until they crash together over everyone's heads. You'll see, no one will stir, and yet there will be a raging storm. It gives me extraordinary pleasure to stage something like that.'

'What do you want to do first?'

'As I've said, I'd like to save that up for later. For the time being it would be enough if we could threaten and beat him into agreeing to anything.'

'To what?' Törless couldn't help saying. They stared each other straight in the eye.

'Oh, don't act the innocent; you know what we're talking about.'

Törless said nothing. Had Reiting discovered something? Was it a shot in the dark?

'. . . You remember, Beineberg's told you what Basini is willing to do.'

Törless sighed with relief.

'Come on, you don't need to make such big eyes. You made them back then, too, and it's not as serious as all that. Incidentally, Beineberg has admitted to me that he gets up to the same thing with Basini.' And Reiting looked over at Beineberg with an ironic grimace. That was his way, tripping someone up, publicly and without the slightest scruple.

But Beineberg did not reply; he stayed where he was, in his thoughtful posture, and barely opened his eyes.

'Aren't you going to come out with it? He's got a deranged plan in mind for Basini, and he wants to take it to its conclusion before we do anything else. It's quite amusing.'

Beineberg remained solemn; he looked at Törless with a thought-ful expression and said, 'Do you remember what we said behind the coats that time?'

'Yes.'

'I've never mentioned it again, because there's no point in mere talk. But I've thought about it often, believe me. And what Reiting just said to you is true. I've got up to the same thing with Basini as he has. I've maybe even gone a bit further. Because, as I said back then, I was convinced that sensuality might be the right approach. It was an experiment. I didn't know any other way of getting what I was after. But there's no point not having plans. I've been thinking – staying awake at night, thinking – about how we might put something systematic in its place.

'Now I think I've found it, and we're going to carry out our experiment. Now you too will see how wrong you were. All the things that are claimed about the world are uncertain, everything happens in a different way. In those days we were coming to it from the reverse side, in a sense, looking for the points where the natural explanation stumbles over its own feet. But now I hope that I will be able to demonstrate the positive aspect – the other side!'

Reiting was handing around the bowls of tea; as he did so he gave Törless a cheerful nudge. 'Pay attention – it's strong stuff, what he's come up with.'

But Beineberg, with a rapid motion, turned out the lamp. In the dark, only the spirit flame of the cooker cast uneasy, bluish lights on the three faces.

'I put out the lamp, Törless, because it's easier to talk about things like that in the dark. And you, Reiting, can go to sleep as far as I'm concerned, if you're too stupid to understand anything more profound.'

Reiting laughed, amused.

'So you remember our conversation. You had discovered that little mathematical curiosity. The example that shows that our thinking doesn't walk on solid, secure, even ground, but rather that it walks over holes. It closes its eyes, it ceases for a moment to exist, and is then transferred safely over to the other side. We should really have despaired long ago, because every area of our knowledge is riddled with such crevasses, nothing but fragments drifting in an unfathomable ocean.

'But we don't despair, we feel as safe as though we were on dry land. If we didn't have that safe, secure feeling, we would kill ourselves in despair at the poverty of our intellect. That feeling is our constant companion, it holds us together, every other moment it protectively takes our intellect in its arms like a little child. Once we have become aware of it, we can no longer deny the soul's existence. Once we dissect our spiritual life and acknowledge the inadequacy of the intellect, we really feel all of this. We feel it – you understand – because if that feeling did not exist, we would collapse like empty sacks.

'We have only forgotten how to pay attention to that feeling, but it is one of the oldest feelings of all. Thousands of years ago people living thousands of miles apart knew of it. Once one begins to deal with these things, they become impossible to deny. But I don't want to persuade you with words; I shall just tell you what you absolutely need to know, so that you are not entirely unprepared. The facts will supply the proof.

'So if we assume the existence of the soul, it's quite obvious that there can be nothing more urgent than that we should re-establish our lost contact with it, familiarize ourselves with it once again, learn how to exploit its powers more effectively, gain for ourselves parts of the supernatural forces slumbering in its depths . . .

'Because all of that is possible, it has been done more than once, the miracles, the saints, the Indian holy men all bear witness to such events –'

'Come on,' Törless interrupted, 'now you're persuading yourself of the truth of those beliefs. That's why you had to turn out the lamp. But would you talk like that if we were now sitting among the others, studying geography and history with them, writing letters home with all the lights full on, and perhaps with the prefect walking around the desks? Wouldn't your words seem a little bizarre, a little presumptuous, as though we didn't belong among the others, as though we were living in another world, eight hundred years earlier?'

'No, my dear Törless, I would assert exactly the same thing. And, by the way, you always make the mistake of looking to see what everyone else is doing; you're not independent enough. Writing letters home! You're thinking of your parents when we're talking about things like this! What makes you think they can even follow us here? We're young, a generation further on, perhaps there are things in store for us that they have never in their lives imagined. I've felt that in myself, at least.

'But what's the point in talking like this; I'll prove it to you.'

After they had been silent for a while, Törless said, 'How are you actually going to go about getting hold of your soul?'

'I'm not going to analyse that for you now, since I'm going to have to do it in front of Basini anyway.'

'You could at least tell me in the meantime.'

'Fine. History teaches us that only a single path leads there: immersion in the self. Except that's the difficult thing. The old saints, for example, back in the time when the soul still expressed itself in miracles, were able to achieve that goal by fervent prayer. The soul must have been different in those days, because that path doesn't work any more. Today, we don't know what to do; the soul has changed, and unfortunately there were times in between when inadequate attention was paid to it and the connection was lost for ever. We can only find a new path by careful reflection. I've been busying myself intensely with that over the last while. Hypnosis should bring us closest to it. But that has never been tried. People only ever try the most everyday tricks, which is why the methods have not been tested to see whether they might lead to anything higher. The last thing I'd say on the subject is that I'm not going to hypnotize Basini in that common-or-garden way, but in a manner of my own devising which, if I'm not mistaken, is similar to one that was used in the Middle Ages.'

'Isn't Beineberg priceless?' laughed Reiting. 'Except he should have lived at the time of the apocalyptic prophecies, and then he would have ended up believing that it was the magic of his soul that saved the world.'

When Törless looked at Beineberg for his response to this mockery, he saw that his face was rigidly distorted as though in a convulsion of attentiveness. The next moment he felt himself being gripped by ice-cold fingers. Törless was alarmed by that level of excitement; then the tension of the hand that gripped him relaxed. 'Oh, it was nothing. Just a thought. I felt as though something special was about to occur to me, an indication of how it should be done . . .'

'Listen, you're getting a bit worked up,' Reiting said jovially; 'you've always been a steely chap and only ever did things like this for fun; but now you're being like a girl.'

'Oh come on – you have no idea what it means to know such things are near by, to be close to possessing them every day.'

'Stop fighting,' said Törless – over the past few weeks he had become much more solid and energetic – 'as far as I'm concerned anyone can do whatever he likes; I don't believe in anything. Neither your worn-out torments, Reiting, nor Beineberg's hopes. And for myself I have nothing to say. I'm just waiting to see what you have up your sleeves.'

'All right, when?'

They decided on the night after next.

Törless did not resist that night's approach. In this new situation, even his feelings for Basini had cooled completely. That was a very fortuitous solution, because at least it freed him at a stroke from the vacillation between shame and desire that he was unable to escape of his own volition. Now at least he had a clear, direct distaste for Basini, as though the humiliations meant for the boy might sully him as well.

Otherwise he was distracted, and unable to think seriously about anything; least of all about what had once so preoccupied him.

Only when he climbed the stairs to the attic with Reiting, Beineberg having already gone on ahead with Basini, did the memory of what had once happened within him become more vivid. He could not get out of his head the cocky words he had hurled at Beineberg on the subject, and he longed to regain that confidence. Hesitantly he held his foot back on each step. But his old certainty wouldn't return. He remembered all the thoughts he had had in those days, but they seemed to pass him by in the distance, as though they were only shadow-pictures of a thought he had once had.

Finally, finding nothing within himself, his curiosity focused once again on the events that were to come from outside, and spurred him onwards.

He hurried up the remaining steps behind Reiting.

While the iron door creaked shut behind them, he felt with a sigh that while Beineberg's plan might be only a ridiculous piece of hocus-pocus, it was at least something solid and considered, while everything within him was in opaque confusion.

They sat down on a crossbeam – in tense excitement, as though they were in the theatre.

Beineberg was already there with Basini.

The situation seemed to favour his plan. The darkness, the stale air, the rotten, sweet smell emanating from the bottles of water, created a feeling that one was drifting off to sleep, never to wake up again, and was certainly not exciting.

Suddenly Beineberg took the revolver out of his pocket and held it against Basini.

Even Reiting leaned forward, to be able to jump between them at any moment.

But Beineberg was smiling. His face was peculiarly distorted, as though he didn't actually want to smile, but some fanatical words surging up inside him had pushed his lips aside.

Basini had fallen to his knees as though paralysed, and stared at the weapon, his eyes wide with fear.

'Stand up,' said Beineberg. 'If you do exactly as I say, no harm will come to you; but if you disturb me with the slightest objection I will shoot you down. Remember that! I am going to kill you anyway, but you will come back to life. Dying isn't as strange to us as you think; we die every day – in deep, dreamless sleep.'

Again the confused smile twisted Beineberg's mouth.

'Now kneel up there,' – there was a broad horizontal beam at waist height – 'like that – bolt upright – keep yourself quite straight – draw your pelvis in. And now keep on staring at it; but without blinking, you must open your eyes as wide as you can.'

Beineberg set a little spirit flame in front of him, so that he had to bend his head back a little to look fully into it.

Little could be seen in the darkness, but after some time Basini's body seemed to start swinging back and forth like a pendulum. The bluish reflections moved up and down on his skin. Every now and again Törless thought he could see Basini's face distorted with fear.

After a while Beineberg asked, 'Are you sleepy?'

The question was put in the usual manner of hypnotists.

Then he began to explain, in a quiet, husky voice:

'Dying is only a consequence of the way we live. We live from one thought to another, from one feeling to the next. Because our thoughts and feelings do not flow peacefully like a stream, they "occur to us", they drop into us like stones. If you observe yourself very carefully, you will feel that the soul is not something that changes its colours in gradual transitions, but rather that thoughts leap forth from it like numbers from a black hole. One moment you have a thought or a feeling, and all of a sudden there's another one there, as though it had sprung from nowhere. If you pay attention, you can even sense the moment between two thoughts when everything is black. That moment – once we have grasped it – is nothing short of death for us.

'For our life consists of nothing but setting out milestones and hopping from one to the next, across a thousand dying seconds every day. In a sense we live only in the pauses in between. That's why we have this ridiculous fear of irrevocable death, because more than anything else it lacks those milestones, it is the immeasurable abyss into which we fall. It is the complete negation of this way of living.

'But only from the perspective of this life, only for someone who has not learned to feel otherwise than from moment to moment.

'This is what I call the "hopping sickness", and the secret lies in overcoming it. We must awaken the feeling of our life as something gliding quietly within ourselves. The moment we succeed in doing that, we are as close to death as we are to life. We have ceased to live – according to our earthly concepts – but we cannot die, either, because in transcending life we have also transcended death. It is the moment of immortality, the moment in which the soul steps out of our narrow brain and into the glorious gardens of its life.

'So follow me very carefully.

'Put all your thoughts to sleep, stare into this little flame . . . don't think from one thing to the next . . . Focus all your attention within yourself . . . Stare at the flame . . . your thought is becoming like a machine that is going slower and slower . . . going . . . slower . . . and slower . . . Stare inside yourself . . . until you find the point where you feel yourself without feeling an idea or a sensation . . .

'Your silence will be my answer. Don't turn your gaze from within . . . !' Minutes passed . . .

'Do you feel that point . . . ?'

No reply.

'Tell me, Basini, have you got there?'

Silence.

Beineberg stood up, and his haggard shadow rose up beside the beam. Up above, Basini's body, drunk with darkness, could be made out swinging back and forth.

'Turn to the side,' ordered Beineberg. 'What is obeying now is only the brain,' he murmured, 'which continues to function mechanically for a while, until the last traces that the soul has impressed upon it are consumed. The soul itself is somewhere – in its next life. It no longer bears the fetters of the natural laws . . .' now he turned to Törless, 'it is no longer condemned to the punishment of making a body heavy, of holding it together. Lean forward, Basini – like that – very gradually . . . further and further out with your body . . . As the final trace in the brain is extinguished, the muscles will relax and the empty body will collapse in on itself. Either that or it will stay floating; I don't know; the soul has left the body by its own power, it is not the ordinary kind of death, perhaps the body remains floating in the air because nothing, no power of life or of death, possesses it any longer ... Lean forward ... even more.'

At that moment Basini's body, which had been obeying all the orders out of fear, clattered heavily to Beineberg's feet.

Basini cried out with pain. Reiting started laughing loudly. But Beineberg, who had taken a step back, emitted a gurgling cry of rage when he had understood the swindle. Moving like lightning, he ripped his leather belt from his body, grabbed Basini by the hair and began madly whipping him. All the terrible tension to which he had been subject flowed into those furious lashings. And Basini howled with pain beneath them, until every corner echoed as though with the lamentation of a howling dog.

Törless had been silent throughout the whole performance. He had quietly hoped that something else might happen, to put him back within the circle of his lost feelings. It was a foolish hope, he had always been aware of that, but still it had held him fast. But now it seemed that everything was over. The scene repelled him. Not an idea in his head; dumb, dead repulsion.

He rose quietly to his feet and left without saying a word.

Beineberg was still whipping away at Basini, and would do until he was exhausted.

When Törless was lying in bed, he felt: 'A conclusion has been reached. Something is over.'

For the next few days he got on quietly with his school work; he didn't worry about anything; Reiting and Beineberg could get on with implementing their programme, one point after another, but Törless kept out of their way.

Then, on the fourth day, when there was no one around, Basini came over to him. He looked miserable, his face was pale and gaunt, in his eyes there flickered the fever of a constant fear. Speaking hastily, with shy sidelong glances, he said, 'You've got to help me! You're the only one who can! I can't bear the way they're torturing me any more. So far I've put up with everything . . . but now they want to beat me to death!'

Törless disliked having to reply to this. Finally he said, 'I can't help you. You yourself are to blame for everything that happens to you.'

'But you were so nice to me not so long ago.'

'Never.'

'But –'

'Shut up about it. That wasn't me . . . A dream . . . A mood . . . I'm even glad that your new disgrace has pulled me away from you . . . It's better for me . . .'

Basini lowered his head. He felt that a sea of grey, sober disappointment had interposed itself between himself and Törless . . . Törless was cold, he had become someone else.

Then he threw himself on his knees in front of him, struck his head on the floor and shouted, 'Help me! Help me! . . . For God's sake, help me!'

Törless hesitated for a moment. He felt neither the desire to help Basini nor sufficient anger to push him away. So he obeyed the first thought that came to him. 'Come to the attic tonight, I want to talk to you about it again.' But he regretted it a moment later.

'Why should I get involved?' it occurred to him, and he said thoughtfully: 'But they would only see you; I can't do it.'

'Oh no, they were up with me all last night, until early in the morning – they'll sleep tonight.'

'All right, then. But don't expect me to help you.'

Törless had arranged to meet Basini contrary to his own convictions, which were that everything inward was over and done with, and there was nothing more to be salvaged. Only a kind of pedantry, a stubborn conscientiousness, hopeless from the start, had whispered to him that he should go back to fiddling around with those events again.

He needed to keep it brief.

Basini didn't know how he should behave. He had taken such a thrashing that he barely dared move. Every trace of personality seemed to have vanished from him; only in his eyes a remnant of it huddled together, and seemed to cling, fearful and pleading, to Törless.

He waited to see what Törless would do.

Finally Törless broke the silence. He spoke quickly, in a bored voice, as one does when one is obliged to carry out once again, for form's sake, a task that has long since been laid to rest.

'I'm not going to help you. I did take an interest in you for a while, but that's all over now. You are really nothing but a rotten, cowardly boy. And that's all. Why should I stand up for you? I always used to think that I would find a different word, a different feeling to describe you, but there is really no more descriptive way of putting it than to say you're rotten and cowardly. It's so simple, so meaningless, and yet there's nothing else to be said. I can no longer remember what I used to want from you, since you got in the way of it with your lecherous demands. I wanted to find a point far away from you, to look at you from there . . . that was my interest in you; you yourself destroyed it . . . but enough, I don't owe you an explanation. Just one other thing: how do you feel now?'

'What do you expect me to feel? I can't bear it any more.'

'They're doing horrible things to you and hurting you?'

'Yes.'

'Just pain, though, simple as that? You feel you're suffering and you want to escape it? Simply that, and with no complications?'

Basini couldn't think of an answer.

'Fine, I'm just asking vaguely, I'm not being precise enough. But that doesn't matter. I have nothing more to do with you. You don't make me feel the slightest thing any more. Do whatever you like . . .'

Törless was on the point of going.

Then Basini tore the clothes from his body and pressed himself against Törless. His body was covered all over with lashes – repellent. His movements were wretched, like those of an ungainly prostitute. Nauseated, Törless turned away.

But he had barely taken the first few steps into the dark when he bumped into Reiting.

'What's all this, are you having secret rendezvous with Basini?'

Törless followed Reiting's gaze and looked back at Basini. A broad beam of moonlight fell in through a skylight at the precise point where the boy was standing. In it, the weals on Basini's bluish skin looked like a leper's sores. Törless automatically tried to apologize for the sight.

'He asked me to.'

'What does he want?'

'He wants me to protect him.'

'Then he's come to the right person.'

'Maybe I will, but I'm fed up with the whole thing.'

Reiting gave him a look of unpleasant consternation, then angrily turned on Basini.

'We'll teach you to conspire against us! Your guardian angel Törless will watch, and it will give him pleasure.'

Törless had already turned away, but this malicious remark, clearly aimed at him, held him back without his thinking about it.

'Listen, Reiting, I'm not going to do that. I don't want anything more to do with it; I find the whole thing repellent.'

'All of a sudden?'

'Yes, all of a sudden. Because before, I was looking for something behind it all . . .' Why was that idea forever coming back to him now . . . !

'Aha, second sight.'

'That's right; but now all I can see is that you and Beineberg are stale and coarse.'

'Oh, just wait and you'll see Basini eating filth,' Reiting joked.

'I'm not interested in that any more.'

'You were, though . . . !'

'I told you ages ago, only as long as Basini's state of mind was a mystery.'

'And now?'

'Now I know nothing about mysteries. Things happen: that's wisdom in its entirety.' Törless was amazed that all of a sudden he was thinking of metaphors that came close to his lost circle of feelings. When Reiting mockingly replied that that was a wisdom one didn't have to go too far to find, an angry feeling of superiority welled up in him, putting harsh words on his lips. For a moment he despised Reiting so much that he would have liked to kick him.

'You can mock; but what you two are doing now is nothing but thoughtless, dreary, disgusting torture!'

Reiting cast a sidelong glance at the listening Basini.

'Restrain yourself, Törless!'

'Disgusting, filthy – you heard me!'

Now it was Reiting's turn to lose his temper.

'I forbid you to slander us here in front of Basini!'

'Come off it. You can't forbid a thing! That time is past. Once I had respect for you and Beineberg, but now I see what you are in comparison to myself. Dull, repellent, beastly fools!'

'Shut your mouth, or . . . !!' Reiting looked as though he was about to leap at Törless. Törless took a step back and shouted at him:

'Do you think I'm going to fight you? As far as I'm concerned, Basini isn't worth it. Do what you want with him, but right now let me pass.'

Reiting seemed to have thought better of lashing out and stepped aside. He didn't even touch Basini. But Törless knew him, and knew that a malicious danger would now be waiting in the wings.

Two days later, in the afternoon, Reiting and Beineberg came up to Törless.

He noticed the wicked look in their eyes. Beineberg clearly held him to blame for the ridiculous collapse of his prophecies, and it seemed likely that Reiting might have had a word with him as well.

'I've heard that you've been slandering us, and that you've been doing it in front of Basini. Why?'

Törless didn't reply.

'You know we won't put up with that kind of thing. But because it's you, and because we're used to your capricious notions and we don't set too much store by them, we're going to let it go. There's only one thing you have to do.' Despite the friendly words, something wicked lurked in Beineberg's eyes.

'Basini's coming to the storeroom tonight; we're going to discipline him for provoking you. When you see us leave, come after us.'

But Törless said no. 'You can do what you like; just leave me out of it.'

'We're going to have fun with Basini once again tonight, and tomorrow we're going to hand him over to the class, because he's starting to act up.'

'Do whatever you want.'

'But you'll be there.'

'No.'

'It's specifically in front of you that Basini must see that nothing can help him against us. Yesterday he was even refusing to carry out our orders; we beat him half to death and he stuck to his guns. We're going to have to return to our moral methods and humiliate him, first in front of you, then in front of the class.'

'But I'm not going to be there!'

'Why?'

'No.'

Beineberg took a deep breath; he looked as though he was trying to collect poison on his lips, then he stepped very close to Törless.

'Do you really think we don't know why? Do you think we don't know how involved you've become with Basini?'

'No more than you two.'

'I see. And that's why he chose you as his special protector? What? – You're trying to tell me he's put his great trust in you? You can't think we're as stupid as that.'

Törless became angry. 'Know what you will, but right now leave me in peace away from your dirty affairs.'

'Are you being cheeky again?'

'You make me sick! Your nastiness is meaningless. That's the repellent thing about you.'

'Listen here, then. You have a lot of things to thank us for. If you think you can lift yourself above us in spite of that, in spite of the fact that we were your teachers, you're making a serious mistake. Are you coming tonight or not?'

'No!'

'My dear Törless, if you rebel against us and don't come, the same thing that happened to Basini will happen to you. You know the situation Reiting found you in. That's enough. We'll turn everyone against you. You're far too stupid and irresolute to be a match for us.

'So if you don't come to your senses in time we'll present you to the class as a fellow culprit along with Basini. Then you can look to him to protect you. Is that understood?'

This flood of threats, coming sometimes from Beineberg, sometimes from Reiting, sometimes from both at once, swept over Törless like a storm. When they had gone, he rubbed his eyes as though he had been dreaming. But he knew Reiting; when angry, he was capable of the vilest actions, and Törless's insults and defiance seemed to have injured him deeply. And Beineberg? He had looked as though he was trembling under a hatred that he had kept in check for years ... and all because he had made a fool of himself in front of Törless.

But the more tragically the events closed over his head, the more indifferent and mechanical they seemed to Törless. He was afraid of the threats. That much was true; but nothing more. The danger had pulled him into the centre of the whirlpool of reality.

He lay down in bed. He saw Beineberg and Reiting going away and Basini's weary footsteps slouching past. But he didn't go with them.

Yet he was tormented by terrible images. For the first time in a while he thought, with some intensity, of his parents. He felt he needed that calm, sure soil if he was to strengthen and ripen that thing which had hitherto brought him nothing but embarrassment.

But what was that thing? He had no time to think about it and dig over what had happened. He felt only a passionate longing to leave behind those confused, troubling relationships; he had a longing for silence, for books. As though his soul was black earth, beneath which the seeds are stirring, and no one knows how they will break forth. The image of a gardener occurred to him, watering his flower-beds each morning, with even, expectant care. That image wouldn't let him go, its expectant certainty seemed to attract all his yearning to itself. That was the only way it could be! The only way! This was what Törless felt, and all his fear, all his reservations, were swept aside by the conviction that he must stake everything on achieving that state of mind.

But he was not clear what would have to happen first. Because more than anything else that longing for peaceful contemplation only intensified his revulsion for the approaching intrigues. He was also truly frightened of the revenge that lay in wait for him. If the other two boys really did try to blacken his name in front of the class, it would take him a huge amount of energy to counter that; and energy was something he did not have to spare. And merely to think of that confusion, that collision with the intentions and the willpower of other people, free of any superior value, made him shudder with disgust.

Then he remembered a letter that he had received from home long before. It was the reply to a letter that he had sent his parents, in which he had, to the best of his ability, told them of his strange states of mind, even before his encounter with his sensuality. Once again it had been a very homespun reply, filled with tired and respectable ethics, and advising him to persuade Basini to stand up for himself, so that his degrading, dangerous state of dependence might come to an end.

Törless had later reread that letter while Basini lay naked beside him on the soft blankets in the hideaway. And it had given him particular pleasure to let those ponderous, simple, plain words melt on his tongue, while reflecting that his parents were blinded by the brightness of their own existence to the darkness in which his soul now crouched like a lithe and feline beast of prey.

But today he approached that passage with quite different feelings.

A pleasant feeling of relief spread out upon him, as though he felt the touch of a firm, benevolent hand. At that moment he had made his decision. A thought had flashed within him, and he had seized it without a thought, as if under his parents' patronage.

He lay awake until the three returned. Then he waited until he could tell from their even breathing that they were asleep. Now he quickly tore a page from his notebook and wrote upon it in the uncertain light of his bedside lamp, in large, unsteady letters:

'They are going to hand you over to the class tomorrow, and there are terrible things in store for you. The only way out is to go to the head and confess. He is going to get to hear about it anyway, except that they would beat you half to death beforehand.

'Blame R. and B. for everything and say nothing about me.

'You can see that I'm trying to save you.'

He put this piece of paper into the sleeping boy's hand.

Then he too, exhausted with excitement, fell asleep.

Beineberg and Reiting seemed to want to grant Törless the next day as grace.

But matters with Basini were becoming serious.

Törless saw Beineberg and Reiting walking over to individual boys, and saw eagerly whispering groups forming around them.

He didn't know whether Basini had found the piece of paper because he had had no opportunity to ask, feeling as he did that he was under observation.

At first he was afraid that they might be talking about him as well. But so paralysed was he by the repulsiveness of the danger that he would not have put up the slightest resistance.

Only later did he timidly mingle with one of the groups, prepared for them all to round on him in an instant.

But no one noticed him at all. Their sole concern was Basini.

The excitement grew, as Törless was able to observe. Reiting and Beineberg might have spiced it up with some lies . . .

At first they only smiled, then some of them grew serious, and hostile glances were darted at Basini. Finally, hot, dark and filled with dark desires, an oppressive silence descended upon the classroom.

It happened to be a free afternoon.

They all gathered at the back by the lockers; then Basini was called to the front.

Beineberg and Reiting stood on either side of him like animal-tamers.

After the doors had been locked and sentries posted, the well-tried method of stripping his clothes off made for general amusement.

Reiting held a little packet of letters from Basini's mother to her son in his hand and began to read.

'My dear, good child . . .'

General roaring.

'You know that of the little money that I have as a widow . . .'

Obscene laughter, bawdy jokes float up from the crowd. Reiting tries to go on reading. Suddenly someone gives Basini a shove. He falls on someone else, who pushes him back, half joking, half in earnest. A third passes him on. And suddenly Basini is flying around the room, naked, his mouth wide with fear, like a rolling ball, amidst laughter and jeering, clutching hands – from one side to the other – cutting himself open on the sharp edges of the desks, falling to his knees, torn bloody – and finally collapsing bleeding and dusty, with glazed, animal eyes as a moment of silence falls and everyone presses forward to see him lying on the floor.

Törless shuddered. He had seen the power of the terrible threat made reality.

And he still didn't know what Basini would do.

The next night Basini was to be tied to a bed and whipped with the blades of foils.

But to the general amazement the headmaster appeared in class early the next morning. He was accompanied by the form master and two other teachers. Basini was removed from the class and brought to a room of his own.

But the headmaster delivered a furious address about brutalities that had come to light, and ordered a strict investigation.

Basini had given himself up.

Someone must have told him about what was in store.

No one suspected Törless. He sat still, turned in on himself, as though the whole business had nothing to do with him.

Not even Reiting and Beineberg suspected him of betrayal. They hadn't even meant their threats to him seriously; they had been uttered to intimidate him, to make him feel their superiority, and perhaps out of irritation; now that their anger had passed they barely gave them a thought. Even their obligations to his parents would have kept them from engaging in any action against Törless. That was so obvious to them that they could not imagine any retaliation on his part.

Törless felt no regret at the step he had taken. The secrecy and cowardice attached to it were nothing in comparison with his feeling of total liberation. After all the excitement, he now had a wonderful feeling of clarity and space.

He took no part in the agitated conversations about what was to come, which were being held all around him; all day he just got on quietly with his life.

When evening came and the lamps were lit he sat at his desk, setting in front of him the notebook in which he had jotted down those hasty notes.

But he did not read it for long. He ran his hand over the pages and it seemed to him as though a faint scent was rising from them, like the fragrance of lavender from old letters. It was the tenderness mingled with melancholy which we bring to a time that belongs irrevocably to the past, when a pale, delicate shadow rises from it bearing the lilies of the dead, and in it we find a forgotten likeness to ourselves.

And that faint, wistful shadow, that pale scent, seemed to vanish away into a wide, full, warm stream – the life that now lay open before him.

A stage of development had reached its conclusion, the soul had begun a new ring like a young tree, and that silent, overwhelming feeling excused everything that had happened.

Now Törless began to flick through the notes he had made. The sentences in which he had helplessly recorded events – that multifarious astonishment, that sense of being affected by life – came alive again, began to stir and become coherent. They lay before him like a bright path bearing the imprints of his tentative footsteps. But still they seemed to be missing something; not a new thought, it wasn't that; but they did not yet come fully alive for him.

He felt unsure of himself. And now he grew anxious about standing before his teachers tomorrow and having to justify himself. How? How would he explain it to them? How could he explain the dark, mysterious path that he had taken? If they asked him why he had mistreated Basini he wouldn't be able to answer: Because I was interested in a process in my brain, something which, in spite of everything, I still don't really understand, something that makes what I think about it seem quite unimportant in comparison.

That small step, which still separated him from the final point on the spiritual process he had to undergo, frightened him like a terrible abyss.

And before nightfall Törless was in a state of feverish, fearful excitement.

The next day, when the pupils were called for questioning one by one, Törless had disappeared.

He had last been seen the previous evening, sitting over a notebook, apparently reading.

They looked throughout the institute, Beineberg sneaked up to look in the storeroom, and Törless was nowhere to be found.

It soon became clear that he had fled the school, and the proper authorities in all the surrounding districts were alerted to bring him back with all due care.

Meanwhile the investigation began.

Reiting and Beineberg, who believed that Törless had fled for fear that he might be implicated, now felt obliged to shift all suspicion away from him, and spoke up violently on his behalf.

They heaped all the guilt on Basini, and the entire class, one by one, testified that Basini was a thieving good-for-nothing who had responded to the most well-meaning attempts to make him mend his ways by repeating the offence. Reiting asserted that they saw they had made a mistake, but they had only done it because pity dictated that one should not deliver a schoolmate up to punishment before all the means of benign instruction had been exhausted, and once again the whole class swore that Basini's mistreatment boiled over only because Basini had responded with the most dreadful, the vilest scorn to those who were, out of the most noble sentiments, attempting to spare him.

In short, it was a well-organized farce, brilliantly staged by Reiting, and by way of excuse it struck every moral note that was likely to find favour with the teachers.

Basini maintained a dull-witted silence. He was still in a state of terror from the events of two days before, and the solitude of his confinement and the calm, businesslike progress of the investigation were already a relief to him. He desired nothing but a rapid conclusion. And Reiting had not neglected to threaten him with the most terrible revenge if he spoke out against them.

Then Törless was brought in. He had been apprehended, dead tired and hungry, in the nearest town.

His flight seemed to be the only mysterious thing about the whole affair. But the situation was in his favour. Beineberg and Reiting had done good groundwork, speaking of the nervous condition that he was thought to have revealed, and his moral sensitivity, which accounted it a crime that he, who knew of everything from the start, had not immediately denounced the affair and was thus partially guilty for the disaster.

So Törless was welcomed with a certain emotional benevolence, and his schoolmates prepared him for it in time.

But he was terribly agitated, utterly exhausted by the fear that he might not be able to make himself understood . . .

For the sake of discretion, since certain revelations were still feared, the investigation was conducted in the headmaster's private apartment. Also present, apart from the headmaster, were the form master, the divinity teacher, and the mathematics master who had, as the youngest staff member, been assigned the duty of taking the minutes.

Asked the reason for his flight, Törless said nothing.

General sympathetic nodding.

'Fine,' said the headmaster, 'we have been informed about that. But tell us what led you to keep Basini's behaviour a secret.'

Törless could now have lied. But his timidity had vanished. He itched to talk about himself and try his thoughts out on them.

'I don't really know, Headmaster. The first time I heard of it, it seemed to me to be something quite terrible . . . something unimaginable . . .'

The divinity teacher gave Törless a gratified and encouraging nod.

'I . . . I thought about Basini's soul . . .'

The divinity teacher beamed, the mathematician cleaned his pince-nez, straightened it, squinted his eyes . . .

'I couldn't imagine the moment when such humiliation had descended upon Basini, and for that reason I felt drawn to his presence time and again . . .'

'I see – you are probably trying to say that you felt a natural revulsion for your classmate's errors, and that the sight of vice enthralled you, as the gaze of snakes is said to do to their victims.'

With lively gestures, the form master and the mathematician hurried to demonstrate their agreement with this simile.

But Törless said, 'No, it wasn't actually revulsion. It was more like this: at one point I said to myself that he had made a mistake, and he should be handed over to the people who would punish him . . .'

'Which is what you should have done.'

'. . . But then it seemed so strange to me that I couldn't think in terms of punishment, and I found myself confronting him from a quite different angle; every time I thought of him something within me cracked . . .'

'You must express yourself more clearly, my dear Törless.'

'It can't be put any other way, Headmaster.'

'Yes it can. You're agitated; we can see that; confused – what you just said was very obscure.'

'Well, yes, I do feel confused; I had found a much better way of putting it. But it all comes down to the same thing, there was something odd happening within me . . .'

'Fine – but that much is quite obvious throughout this whole business.'

Törless reflected for a moment.

'Perhaps I can put it like this: there are certain things that are destined to intervene in our lives in two ways. I have found these to include people, events, dark, dusty corners, a high, cold silent wall that suddenly came alive . . .'

'For goodness' sake, Törless, where are your ramblings taking you?'

But Törless was now enjoying getting everything out of his system.

'. . . imaginary numbers . . .'

They all looked at each other and then at Törless. The mathematician wheezed:

'I must add, if we are to have a better understanding of these obscure statements, that young Törless once visited me to ask me to explain certain fundamental mathematical concepts – including the imaginary – which might in fact present difficulties for the untrained intellect. I must even admit that he developed an undeniably keen perception, but he had a real mania for seeking out only things which seemed to signify – for him at least – a gap in the causality of our thinking. Do you remember, Törless, what you said then?'

'Yes. I said it seemed to me that at those points we were unable to make the crossing with our thought alone, but needed another, more inward certainty, to carry us over. And I felt the same about Basini: we can't get by with thought alone.'

The headmaster was already growing impatient with the philosophical turn that the investigation was taking, but the chaplain was very satisfied with Törless's reply.

'So,' he asked, 'you feel drawn away from science towards religious points of view? It was clearly very similar in the case of Basini,' he said, turning to the others. 'He seems to have a sensitive temperament for the finer things, I should say the divine and transcendental essence of morality.'

Now, though, the headmaster felt obliged to intervene.

'Listen, Törless, is it as the reverend father says? Do you have a tendency to seek a religious background behind events or things, as you expressed it in rather general terms?'

He himself would have been happy if Törless had finally agreed, providing a sound basis for his judgement. But Törless said, 'No, that wasn't it either.'

'Right then, tell us once and for all,' the headmaster exploded, 'what it *was*. We can't possibly get involved in a philosophical debate with you.'

But by now Törless was defiant. He himself felt that he had expressed himself badly, but both the opposition and the wrong-headed agreement he had met with gave him a feeling of arrogant superiority over these older people who seemed to know so little of the human spirit.

'I can't help it if none of it is what you meant. But I can't give a precise account to myself of what I felt on each individual occasion; though if I say what I think about it now, perhaps then you will understand why it took me so long to get free of it.'

He now stood up straight, as proudly as though he was the judge here, and he looked right ahead, past the men. He couldn't bear to look at those ridiculous figures.

Outside the window a crow was sitting on a branch. Otherwise there was nothing but the huge, white plain.

Törless felt that the moment had come when he would speak clearly, distinctly and triumphantly of the things that had been at work within him, at first vague and tormenting, then lifeless and without force.

It was not as though a new thought had given him this certainty, this clarity. As he stood straight in the room, as though there was nothing around him but an empty space – he, his whole being, felt it as he had felt it back then, when his eyes had wandered among his writing, studying, busy classmates.

Because thoughts are something special. Often they are nothing more than accidents that pass away without leaving a trace, and thoughts, too, have their times to live and to die. We can have a flash of insight, and then, slowly, it fades beneath our touch like a flower. The form remains, but the colours, the scent are missing.

We remember them word for word, and the logic of the sentence is completely unimpaired, and yet it drifts ceaselessly around on the surface of our minds and we feel none the richer for it. Until – perhaps several years later – all of a sudden another moment comes when we see that in the meantime we have known nothing of it, although logically we knew everything.

Yes, there are dead and living thoughts. The sort of thinking which moves on the illuminated surface, which can be checked at any point along the thread of causality, does not need to be the living kind. A thought that one encounters along that path remains indifferent, like a man chosen at random from within a column of marching soldiers. A thought – it may have passed through our brain long ago – comes to life only at the moment when it is joined by something that is no longer thought, no longer logical, so that we feel its truth beyond all justification, like an anchor tearing from it into blood-filled, living flesh . . . Any great realization is only half completed in the brain's pool of light; the other half is formed in the dark soil of our innermost being, and above all it is a state of the soul on whose furthest tip the thought sits perched, like a flower.

All Törless had needed was a jolt to the soul to send that final shoot surging into the light.

Without giving a thought to the stunned faces around him, effectively speaking only to himself, he followed on from this and, his eyes focused straight in front of him, brought his speech to its conclusion.

'. . . Perhaps I have not yet learned enough to express myself properly, but I will describe it. It happened within me just now, once again. I cannot put it any other way except to say that I see things in two forms. Everything, thoughts included. They are the same today as they were yesterday, and if I try to find a difference and close my eyes, they come alive in a different light. Perhaps I was wrong about irrational numbers; when I think of them in mathematical terms, so to speak, they are natural to me, while if I consider them directly in all their strangeness, they seem impossible. I may well be mistaken about that, perhaps I know too little about them. But I wasn't mistaken about Basini, I wasn't mistaken when my ear could not turn away from the quiet trickling in the high wall, when my eye could not turn away from the silent life of dust suddenly illuminated by a lamp. No, I wasn't mistaken when I spoke of a second, secret, unnoticed life of things! I – I don't mean it literally – these things aren't alive, Basini didn't really have two faces – it was rather that there was something else within me which wasn't looking at all these things with the eye of reason. Just as I feel that an idea comes to life inside me, I feel also that there is something alive inside me when I look at things, when thoughts fall silent. There is something dark in me, something among all my thoughts, something that I cannot measure with thoughts, a life that can't be expressed in words and which is none the less my life . . .

'That silent life oppressed and stifled me, I was driven to stare it in the face. I suffered from the fear that the whole of our life was like that, and I was only finding out about it piecemeal, here and there . . . oh, I was terribly frightened . . . I felt as though . . .'

These words and similes, far beyond what was appropriate for Törless's years, fell lightly and naturally from his lips in his great excitement, in a moment of almost poetic inspiration. Now he lowered his voice and, as though gripped by his own suffering, he added:

'Now that is past. I know that I was indeed mistaken. I'm not afraid of anything any more. I know: things are things and will remain so for ever; and no doubt I will see them now one way, now another. Now with the eyes of reason, now with those other eyes . . . And I will no longer try to compare the two . . .'

He fell silent. It seemed quite obvious to him that he could now go, and no one stood in his way.

When he was outside, the men who remained behind looked at each other in bafflement.

The headmaster irresolutely wagged his head back and forth.

The form master was the first to break the silence. 'Goodness, it seems our little prophet wanted to deliver us a lecture. But heaven only knows what to make of it all. The excitement! And all that confusion about quite simple things!'

'Receptiveness and spontaneity of thought,' the mathematician agreed. 'It seems that he has placed too much stress on the subjective factor of our experiences, and that confused him and drove him to his obscure metaphors.'

Only the chaplain remained silent. He had caught the word 'soul' cropping up very frequently in Törless's speech, and would have liked to take the boy under his wing.

Though he wasn't quite sure how it was meant.

But the headmaster brought things to a conclusion. 'I don't know what's really going on in that Törless's head, but he's so over overwrought that life in the institute is probably no longer the right thing for him. He needs greater care of his intellectual nourishment than we are able to supply. I don't think that we can shoulder the responsibility for that any longer. Törless should be educated privately; I shall write to his father to that effect.'

Everyone hurried to agree with the respected headmaster's fine suggestion.

'He was really so peculiar that I almost think he has the temperament of an hysteric,' the mathematician said to his neighbour.

At the same time as Törless's parents received the letter from the headmaster, they received another from Törless, asking them to remove him from the school because he no longer felt it was the place for him.

Meanwhile Basini had been expelled. Everything in the school had resumed its normal course.

It had been agreed that Törless would be collected by his mother. He bade indifferent farewells to his classmates. He was already almost beginning to forget their names.

He had never climbed back up to the red storeroom. All of that seemed to lie far, far behind him.

Since Basini's expulsion it was dead. As though the boy who had formed the centre of all those connections had taken them with him when he left.

Something quiet and doubting had come over Törless, but his despair had gone. 'It must just have been intensified by all that secret business with Basini,' he thought to himself. Otherwise there seemed to be no reason for it.

But he was ashamed, the way we are ashamed the morning after a feverish night, when we have seen terrible dangers looming up from every corner of the dark room.

His behaviour before the investigating committee; it struck him as terribly silly. So much fuss! Hadn't they been right? Such fuss over something so trivial! And yet something within him took the sting from his shame. 'I'm sure my behaviour was quite unreasonable,' he reflected, 'and yet the whole thing seems to have had very little to do with my reason.' That, in fact, was his new feeling. He remembered a terrible storm inside himself, and the reasons with which he tried to explain it, which he still sought within himself, were utterly inadequate. 'So it must have been something much more necessary and deep-rooted,' he concluded, 'than anything that can be judged using reason and concepts . . .'

And that which had existed before his passion, which that passion had merely grown over, the actual thing, the problem, would not budge. The mental perspective that he had experienced, alternating between the near and the far. That elusive context which, according to our point of view, gives things and events sudden values which are utterly incomparable and alien to one another . . .

That and everything else – he saw it as being curiously clear and pure – and small. Just as one sees things in the morning, when the first pure sunbeams have dried the perspiration of anxiety, and the table and the cupboard, the enemy and fate, creep back to their natural dimensions.

But a quiet, brooding weariness remains then, and that was what had happened to Törless. He was now able to tell day from night – in fact he had always been able to, and only a massive dream had washed away those boundaries with its flooding tide, and he was ashamed of that confusion. But the memory that things can be otherwise, that there are fine boundaries around human beings, easily erased, that feverish dreams creep around the soul, gnawing away at solid walls and opening up strange alley-ways – that memory too had sunk deep within him and cast pale shadows.

He was unable to explain a great deal of it. But that silence felt delicious, like the certainty of an impregnated body that feels in its blood the gentle pull of the future. And confidence and weariness mingled in Törless . . .

And so he waited quietly and thoughtfully for his farewell . . .

His mother, who had thought she would find an overwrought and confused young man, was struck by his composure.

When they set off for the station, the little wood with Božena's house lay on their right. It looked so insignificant and harmless, a dusty thicket of willow and alder.

Törless remembered how unimaginable his parents' life had been. And he stole a glance at his mother.

'What is it, my son?'

'Nothing, Mama, I was just thinking about something.'

And he breathed in the faintly perfumed fragrance rising from his mother's waist.

FOR THE BEST IN PAPERBACKS, LOOK FOR THE

In every corner of the world, on every subject under the sun, Penguin represents quality and variety—the very best in publishing today.

For complete information about books available from Penguin—including Penguin Classics, Penguin Compass, and Puffins—and how to order them, write to us at the appropriate address below. Please note that for copyright reasons the selection of books varies from country to country.

In the United States: Please write to *Penguin Group (USA), P.O. Box 12289 Dept. B, Newark, New Jersey 07101-5289* or call 1-800-788-6262.

In the United Kingdom: Please write to *Dept. EP, Penguin Books Ltd, Bath Road, Harmondsworth, West Drayton, Middlesex UB7 0DA.*

In Canada: Please write to *Penguin Books Canada Ltd, 90 Eglinton Avenue East, Suite 700, Toronto, Ontario M4P 2Y3.*

In Australia: Please write to *Penguin Books Australia Ltd, P.O. Box 257, Ringwood, Victoria 3134.*

In New Zealand: Please write to *Penguin Books (NZ) Ltd, Private Bag 102902, North Shore Mail Centre, Auckland 10.*

In India: Please write to *Penguin Books India Pvt Ltd, 11 Panchsheel Shopping Centre, Panchsheel Park, New Delhi 110 017.*

In the Netherlands: Please write to *Penguin Books Netherlands bv, Postbus 3507, NL-1001 AH Amsterdam.*

In Germany: Please write to *Penguin Books Deutschland GmbH, Metzlerstrasse 26, 60594 Frankfurt am Main.*

In Spain: Please write to *Penguin Books S. A., Bravo Murillo 19, 1° B, 28015 Madrid.*

In Italy: Please write to *Penguin Italia s.r.l., Via Benedetto Croce 2, 20094 Corsico, Milano.*

In France: Please write to *Penguin France, Le Carré Wilson, 62 rue Benjamin Baillaud, 31500 Toulouse.*

In Japan: Please write to *Penguin Books Japan Ltd, Kaneko Building, 2-3-25 Koraku, Bunkyo-Ku, Tokyo 112.*

In South Africa: Please write to *Penguin Books South Africa (Pty) Ltd, Private Bag X14, Parkview, 2122 Johannesburg.*

Printed in the United States
by Baker & Taylor Publisher Services